"You're going to make amends for what you've done!"

Jordan's voice was restrained, only hinting at the anger Alex could sense beneath the tightly controlled emotions. "Your treachery has almost cost me the lot—the factory, the business, the whole damned lot!"

"I know how bad it all looks," she began, "but Kenny and I had nothing to do with that leak."

"Do you really expect me to believe that?" The words were scornful.

"What exactly are you planning to do, Jordan?" she asked recklessly. "What revenge have you thought up? How are you going to make me pay for this crime I'm supposed to have committed?"

"Marriage—to me."

Jennifer Taylor, Liverpool-born, still lives in Lancashire, though now in beautiful countryside with her husband, son and daughter. She is a chartered librarian and worked for the Liverpool City Libraries for many years. She has always written and has cupboards full of unfinished manuscripts to prove it. When she decided to try romance writing, Jennifer found it far more challenging and enjoyable than her other efforts. She manages to fit her writing into her busy schedule of working, running the house and caring for the children. Her books contain a strong element of humor, as she feels laughter is important to a loving relationship.

GUILTY OF LOVE
Jennifer Taylor

Harlequin Books

TORONTO • NEW YORK • LONDON
AMSTERDAM • PARIS • SYDNEY • HAMBURG
STOCKHOLM • ATHENS • TOKYO • MILAN
MADRID • WARSAW • BUDAPEST • AUCKLAND

Original hardcover edition published in 1992
by Mills & Boon Limited

ISBN 0-373-03252-8

Harlequin Romance first edition February 1993

GUILTY OF LOVE

CHAPTER ONE

'I'M SORRY, Miss Campbell, but I'm sure you can appreciate the bank's concern. Payments on the loan are already three months behind, and I'm afraid there is no way that we can allow things to continue like this. Have you any idea when you will be in a position to bring your account up to date?'

Alex glanced down at her hands, clasping them tightly in her lap so that they wouldn't tremble and betray her nervousness. Ever since the letter requesting her to make an appointment with the manager at the bank had arrived two long days before, she'd been living on a knife-edge, wondering how she would answer that simple question. Yet now that it had been asked, and Mr Simpson was waiting for an answer, she still had no clear idea what to say. If only the nest-egg Mother had left them were still intact there would have been no problem, but Kenny's antics over the past couple of years had put paid to that!

Just for a moment anger at the foolish way her brother had behaved rose hotly inside her before determinedly she pushed it from her mind. Berating Kenny would achieve nothing, as it never did. What she had to concentrate on was finding some way to persuade the bank to give her a bit of breathing-space. She'd worked too hard to get Little Gems up on its feet to sit back now and watch it stagger to its knees. She would find the money to make up the missing payments somehow... she would!

'Frankly, Mr Simpson, I don't see that there is that much of a problem. Oh, I know there are three payments outstanding, but in terms of hard cash it is a small amount compared to the turnover the shop is doing.' Her tone was perfect—cool, faintly amused, as though she couldn't quite understand why the bank should be making such a fuss over something so trivial; but it appeared that Mr Simpson wasn't going to fall in line quite as she'd hoped.

'Agreed, Miss Campbell, but I have your statements here for the past quarter's trading and, although as you say the shop is producing a healthy turnover, your outgoings have tended to outweigh your credits quite considerably.'

He passed a printed sheet across the desk, but Alex had no need to read the neatly totalled columns of figures. She knew to a penny how much money she'd paid out over the past few months, knew also that there was no way it could continue when she was already experiencing difficulty in paying suppliers.

Although she designed and made the more expensive items of jewellery which gave the shop its edge over competitors, it was the cheaper lines she bought in from the wholesalers which were her bread and butter. Still, now that she had finally managed to pay off Kenny's gambling debts, she should be able to plough all the profit back into the business. With Christmas and all the extra trade it brought just a couple of months away, she should be able to reverse the losses and catch up on the payments.

'You're quite right, Mr Simpson. I have had rather a lot of expenditure recently, but I assure you that won't need to continue. I know it's asking a lot, but if the bank would give me a few weeks' grace, then I am confident that I can catch up on the missing payments.'

'Well...' Mr Simpson hesitated, obviously torn between a desire to help and a need to safeguard the bank's interests, and Alex decided to give him a little push in the right direction. Leaning forwards across the desk, she gave him her most radiant smile, her blue eyes soft and luminous.

'Please, Mr Simpson. I know it has been most remiss of me to let this happen, but I'm certain that, with your... the bank's help, I can sort everything out.'

'I—er——' Obviously deeply affected by both the smile and the softly beguiling tone, he ran a finger round inside his collar, his face a trifle flushed. Alex tried hard not to gloat as she sat back in her seat. She'd learned at a very tender age that even the strongest men tended to weaken when she looked at them with that helpless little gaze. She might be a modern woman, well able to take care of herself in most situations, but what was the point in being female if one didn't make use of one's natural assets? She only had to glance in a mirror to know that with her long blonde hair curling softly round her face and her huge blue eyes she looked delicate and helpless. It was by the way that she was actually neither one of those!

Mr Simpson cleared his throat, obviously making an effort to get himself in hand. 'You really should have come to me the very minute you knew you had a problem, Miss Campbell. We could have worked something out. You must never forget that I—I mean, the bank—is here to help, my dear.'

Alex nearly choked as she swallowed the chuckle of laughter his words evoked, trying to imagine staid Mr Simpson's reaction if she had gone to him for advice... on how to pay off the thugs who were threatening to put Kenny six feet under for welshing on his gambling debts! Still, the offer had been kindly meant, and she was grateful.

'I shall remember that, Mr Simpson. Thank you. However, I do want to assure you that this won't happen again.'

'I'm sure it won't, Miss Campbell. Frankly, I was most surprised when your account was brought to my attention. You have always handled your business in an exemplary manner up to now, and it is for that reason that I shall recommend to head office that we should give you a further three months to make up the back payments.' He glanced at his desk diary. 'Let's say the end of January, shall we?'

'That would be marvellous. Thank you,' Alex said quickly, mentally totting up figures. By her reckonings she should just do it... if she didn't spend an extra penny, or even *think* about celebrating Christmas! Damn Kenny! He was old enough to know better, and this was the last time she would ever bail him out!

She left the bank, turning up the collar of her thick cherry-red coat as she hurried through the throngs of shoppers. It was market day, and Ormskirk was busy under an early October sky, but she bypassed the tempting array of goods. There would be no money over to spend on anything but necessities for the next few months, which was annoying when the shop had been doing so well of late. Now it would be at least a year before she could get it back on to a solid footing. When would Kenny ever learn to control his impulsive behaviour? He might be her twin, but sometimes she felt years older than him. Thank heavens he had managed to hang on to his job at Lang's at least. A couple of months back, when he'd had that run-in with Jordan Lang, the owner of the company, she'd thought he'd blown it; but he'd been lucky. Lang had quite uncharacteristically let him off the hook with just a severe warning. Now they would need every penny Kenny earned as well as what she could make from the shop to pay off this debt. This was definitely the last time she was going to risk everything to save his skin!

The rest of the day passed swiftly enough. There was a steady flow of customers in the shop, and Alex took two more orders for her special lines—one for the topaz scarf-clip, which had recently been featured in one of the leading fashion magazines, and one for her aquamarine waterfall earrings. Although she had made both designs several times before, each item would be slightly different when it was finished, ensuring a degree of individuality. It was the thing which made her jewellery so sought after both in the town and further afield. Every week a percentage of what she made was earmarked for one of the large London stores which were now commissioning her on a regular basis. It had taken years of hard work to get her to this point on the ladder, and there was no way she was prepared to slip down a rung or two. She would find the money to pay the bank what she owed even if it meant starving in the proverbial garret!

By the time she locked up the shop, she could feel her head humming with tension. She set the alarms, then walked through the workroom and up the stairs to the flat she shared with Kenny. Lang's was situated on the other side of town, on the outskirts of Southport, so it would be another hour or more before Kenny made it through the rush-hour traffic. Maybe she would take a couple of aspirin and lie down for a while before starting on supper. She wanted a clear head tonight to make Kenny realise exactly what he had to do to help get them out of this mess he'd created!

She awoke slowly, groaning as her cramped muscles ached in protest when she sat up. Everywhere was dark, and for a moment she felt strangely disorientated until she realised that she must have dozed off on the living-room sofa. She struggled to her feet, and switched on the light, gasping in shock as she caught sight of the figure slumped in the chair.

'Kenny! Lord above, but you gave me a fright! Why didn't you wake me when you got in? What time is it?' Rubbing the sleep from her eyes, she glanced at her watch. 'Seven o'clock! I must have been more tired than I thought. I'll go and make a start on supper because you and I have some serious talking to do tonight.'

She started for the kitchen, her footsteps slowing when she became aware of the unnatural silence in the room. She glanced around, her eyes going immediately to her brother's face, and something in his expression made her go cold in apprehension.

'What is it, Kenny? What's happened?'

He jumped at the harsh note in her voice, and just for an instant he met her eyes, before dropping his gaze back to the carpet. Alex felt the apprehension turn to fear. How many times had she seen that expression on his face when he'd got himself into some scrape or another? She'd lost count, just as she'd lost count of the number of times she'd bailed him out. But not now, please heaven, not now, when everything was so finely balanced. All it would take now was just one little push and they would be hurtling towards disaster!

On leaden legs she walked back across the room and sat down again. 'Just tell me what's happened, Kenny,' she ordered a shade more gently.

'I'm sorry, Lexie, really I am. I didn't plan it. You've got to believe me.'

'Didn't plan what?' She grasped his hands and shook him roughly. 'Listen, Kenny, you have to get a grip on yourself and tell me what you've done, otherwise I won't be able to help you.'

He laughed, a harsh, rasping sound which echoed round the room and made Alex wince. 'I don't think you can this time. I don't think anyone can!'

'Don't be so melodramatic,' she ordered sharply, feeling her stomach lurch at the absolute conviction in his voice. 'It can't be that bad. What have you done?'

'Taken the blueprints for the new engine.'

'The blueprints...? No!' She leapt to her feet, seeing the betraying, guilty colour flood Kenny's face. 'Why? Why did you do such a stupid thing?'

He shrugged, his mouth taking on a sulky line of defiance. 'I didn't plan on doing it. It just sort of happened. I was in old Morgan's office. You know him, the chief designer on the project. He's the one who got me into all that trouble a couple of months back by reporting me to Jordan Lang for talking about the project in the pub. Anyway, I was in his office collecting some data sheets when Morgan was called away. All that talk about the need for security, and that dressing down I got from Lang! That's a laugh! Morgan just walked out of that office without a thought for locking the safe. I could see the blueprints lying there and, well, I don't know. It was just an impulse to take them, I guess. I thought it would teach them all a lesson, and make them realise that anyone can make a mistake.'

'Oh, Kenny, how could you?'

Alex sank weakly down on to the chair, scarcely able to believe what she was hearing. Kenny should have learned his lesson from the last time, when Jordan Lang had hauled him over the coals and threatened him with immediate dismissal if anything else happened; and everyone in the district knew that Lang didn't make threats idly! He ran the engineering company with an iron hand, permitting no quarter to anyone who crossed him. She could understand only too well why Kenny was looking so shaken. The pity was he hadn't stopped to think about what he was doing sooner!

'I'm sorry, Lexie. I know it was a stupid thing to do, but it was just an impulse. Oh, maybe I did have some vague idea at the back of my mind about taking the plans to one of our competitors, and seeing what they'd be willing to pay for them—but that was all it was...a vague idea, even though God knows we need the money.'

'Not that much we don't! Don't you realise how serious this is? It's industrial espionage! You could go to prison for this, Kenny!'

'I know, I know. I must have been mad to even think about it. I realised how crazy it was once I'd had a chance to think things through, but it was too late by then to put the blueprints back. Morgan had left on some sort of urgent business, and his office was all locked up. I suppose in one way I was lucky he did go shooting off and never had time to notice the plans were missing.'

'But what are you going to do now?' Alex asked, trying desperately to stay calm, although it was difficult. Kenny had been in some scrapes in his time, but never anything as serious as this.

'I'll have to put the prints back somehow. If Jordan Lang finds out they're missing, then it won't just be a question of calling the police, believe me. The man's barely civilised when it comes to the well-being of his precious company! He would want his revenge to be far more personal!'

A shudder rippled through Kenny's spare frame at the thought of his formidable employer. He glanced up, a beseeching expression on his strained face. 'You've got to help me, Lexie. You're the only one I can turn to now!'

'How? Even if I agree to try, which I haven't, how can I help?'

Kenny bent down, pulled a long roll of paper from under the chair, and laid it on the coffee-table between them. Alex stared at it in silence, according it the same disgusted fascination she might have a rattlesnake, only she had the nasty feeling that this innocuous roll of paper could prove to be far more dangerous.

'It's simple, really. I've got it all worked out, and I'm sure we can do it.' Kenny adopted the soothing tone she recognised only too well, and Alex steeled herself for the punch line she knew was coming. 'All you have to do is help me put them back tonight before Lang finds out they are missing.'

No! She wanted to scream the word aloud, to shout her refusal so that there could be no misunderstanding; but it was impossible. The bond between her and Kenny was far too strong for her to ever refuse to help him.

The wind was bitter, knifing through the thick folds of the leather flying-jacket and jeans Kenny had insisted she should wear. Turning up the collar of the jacket, Alex huddled down into its fleecy warmth, feeling her stomach churning as though she were on a roller-coaster.

'Right, that should do it. The security staff should be going for their meal-break around now, leaving just one man on duty at the front door. Time to go.'

Pulling the sleeve of his jacket back down over his watch, Kenny re-started the motorbike, then shot Alex a worried look. 'Now, are you sure you know what to do?'

She nodded, not trusting herself to speak because her teeth were chattering, and hearing such indisputable evidence of her fear would make her feel worse than ever.

'Good girl. I know you can do it, Sis, and I give you my word this will be the last time I drag you into anything like this.'

He reached out and gave her trembling fingers a quick squeeze, then swung the motorbike through the gates leading to the factory, and drove steadily along the drive. Alex counted to ten, as he'd instructed her to do, then hurried after him, keeping to the shadows and praying that Kenny had been right in his assessment that anyone looking out of the windows would focus on the bright glare from the bike's headlamp and not on her. As quickly as she could she took up her position behind some bushes close to the front doors of the factory, then waved to Kenny to indicate she was ready, watching with thumping heart as he rang the bell to summon the security guard.

'Evening, Sid. Sorry to bother you, but can you let me into the office? I think I must have left my wallet behind because I can't seem to find it anywhere.'

Kenny sounded relaxed enough, but Alex could see the betraying tension in the set of his body, and held her breath. So much depended on his ability to convince the guard.

'Well, I don't know, Kenny. I'd like to help you, of course, but you know yourself how Lang has tightened up on security over the past couple of months. I don't know if I dare risk it. He'd have my guts for garters if he ever found out I'd gone against his instructions. You know what he can be like!'

There was no mistaking Sid's reluctance, and Alex didn't know whether to be relieved or sorry. Obviously he was just as wary of the formidable Jordan Lang as Kenny was, and suddenly she wasn't so certain that entering the building was the wisest thing to do. If Jordan Lang ever found out about it, then there wasn't even the slimmest chance that he would view it as two wrongs making one nice, tidy right! However, obviously Kenny didn't share her sudden doubts.

'I understand, Sid. I never should have asked and put you on the spot like that. Forget it. I'll manage somehow. Pity, though; I had been going to try that little place out in Burscough you've been telling me about. There's this girl, you see, rather special, and I thought... Never mind. I'm sure she'll understand.'

Kenny half turned to go, his shoulders slumped in dejection, and, if Alex hadn't known what an accomplished actor he could be when he chose to, she would have felt sorry for him herself. It was little wonder that poor old Sid fell for it hook, line and sinker!

'Hang on there, Kenny, son. I don't want to spoil your night. I'll let you in just this once, but make sure no one gets to hear about it. I'll get the sack if Lang ever finds out!'

'You can rely on me, Sid. He won't find out. I can guarantee it!'

The voices faded, and Alex slumped against the wall in a state midway between elation and despair. It seemed that part one of the Great Master Plan was up and running just as Kenny had predicted; now there was nothing standing in the way of part two... and *that* was where she came in!

Forcing herself to stay calm, she settled down to wait, blowing on her hands to warm her numbed fingers before tucking them under her arms to retain a meagre bit of warmth. The blueprints tucked inside her jacket crackled, poking uncomfortably through the soft folds of her sweater to scratch her skin, and she wriggled uncomfortably. It was hard to imagine that a few sheets of paper were worth so much that a man would go to almost any lengths to ensure their safety, but the fear she'd heard in Kenny's voice when he'd spoken of Jordan Lang had been matched by that she'd just heard in Sid's. 'Barely civilised' was how Kenny had described the man. At the time Alex had taken little notice of the remark, but now, standing hidden in the bushes outside the factory, she felt a shiver ripple down her spine which owed little to the biting cold. All she could hope was that she would never have occasion to see if that description matched!

'For heaven's sake, Lexie, stop daydreaming! Come on.'

Alex jumped when she heard her brother hiss her name in an anxious whisper. She fought her way free of the prickly den, and hurried into the building, blinking in the bright glare of the foyer lights.

'Now hurry up. Sid's checking the cloakroom for my wallet, but we haven't got long. I told him I would just run downstairs and phone you to see if you'd found it at home.' He reached across the reception desk and unhooked a key, pressing it into her trembling fingers. 'This is the key to Morgan's office. Remember what I told you: second floor, fifth door along on the right. Just leave the blueprints on the desk, and he'll think he forgot to put them away before he left, and be too embarrassed to say anything.'

'And how do I get out again? You won't be able to keep Sid upstairs much longer.' She glanced round the brightly lit foyer, her whole body shaking with an attack of nerves. She wasn't cut out for this kind of thing; she really wasn't. She was a jeweller, not some kind of cat burglar!

'There's no problem about that. After you've left the prints, go straight along the corridor, and you'll see a fire exit. It's never locked as it can only be opened from the inside. I'll meet you back by the front gate. Piece of cake, really, when you think about it!'

Obviously Kenny's confidence was returning, but Alex just glared at him. 'Piece of cake' indeed! However, now was not the time to debate the point, much as she'd like to. She ran towards the stairs, her soft-soled trainers making little sound on the marble flooring. As fast as she could she made her way up to the second level, then ran along the corridor counting doors until she arrived at the fifth. Just for a moment she hesitated, aware that until she actually unlocked that door she hadn't really committed a crime, then, with a shrug of resignation, slipped the key into the lock. There was no going back now. It was her future at stake as much as Kenny's.

The room was in darkness, and Alex waited until she had closed the door before snapping on the torch she'd brought with her. Swinging the beam around the room to get her bearings, she spotted the desk and hurried towards it, unzipping the front of her jacket to pull out the blueprints. They were very creased from being squashed inside the coat, and she tried to smooth them out, cursing softly when some of the rolls of paper slid out from the middle. Hands shaking, she bent down and un-furled the whole roll to fit the section back into place, then felt herself go cold with shock when the door opened abruptly and the light was switched on.

It was hard to say who was the most surprised, Alex or the tall, dark-haired man who'd just entered the room; but it wasn't hard to say who re-covered first. Alex stood up slowly, her eyes huge in her ashen face as she watched the surprise turn to something else, something which made her knees turn to water. All of a sudden she understood exactly what Kenny had meant, and she felt her heart start to hammer in a sickening heavy rhythm.

With his face all hard angles, his grey eyes glit-tering, and a strange little twist to his lips, there was nothing civilised about Jordan Lang at all!

The sharp click of the lock sounded loud as gunfire in the silence. Alex jumped then shrank back as Jordan Lang closed the door and came further into the room, stopping just a few feet away from her. Slowly he let his gaze run over her from top to toe, then smiled, a slow curving of his lips which did little to quell her mounting fear.

'So...what have we here?'

His voice was low, holding a note of quiet menace which was far more scary than any show of anger might have been, and Alex felt a cold shudder tiptoe its way down her spine.

'Cat got your tongue, then, or have you decided it might be wiser to wait and see what I intend to do before you speak?' He laughed harshly, and Alex shrank back a little further so that she could feel the coldness of the wall against her back. 'That's the hundred-dollar question, isn't it? What am I going to do now? I suppose that depends on your story. So come along; help me decide what I should do next.'

He stood and watched her, one dark brow raised in mocking enquiry, and Alex ran the tip of her tongue over her parched lips while she tried desperately to think up a reason to explain her presence in the office.

'I'm still waiting,' he prompted, almost gently, but one glance at his expression was enough to convince her that being gentle was the furthest thing from Jordan Lang's mind! She swallowed hard, forcing some moisture down her parched throat, her voice strained and raspy when she finally spoke.

'I guess it does seem odd, my being here.'

'Very odd,' he said drily, his eyes catching hers and holding them in his gaze. 'But I'm sure you must have some sort of an explanation for your visit.'

'Of course I have.' She looked away, staring down at the carpet, looking anywhere but into those cold grey eyes.

'Then don't be shy. I can hardly wait to hear it.' He folded his arms across his chest and rested a hip against the edge of the desk, his expression one of cruel mockery, which spurred her into speech.

'It isn't what you think,' she began desperately.

'No? But how can you be sure of that? I mean, I haven't said a word about what I think you're doing here, so how do you know what my views are?'

'It's quite obvious! You think I came here to-night to steal, but you're wrong... quite wrong!'

'Then I suggest you set me right, and tell my why you *are* here.' He glanced at the wafer-thin gold watch strapped to his wrist, then back at her, his grey eyes hard and uncompromising. 'It seems late to be in the office on legitimate business, but I'm prepared to give you the benefit of the doubt and listen to your story.'

He sounded almost reasonable, but one glance at the cold condemnation in his eyes told another story, and Alex felt her temper rise. He had found her guilty in his own mind without even waiting to hear any explanation she might give; but there was no way she was going to stand here and let him class her as a thief!

'I don't like how your mind works, Mr Lang! I'm no thief. I came here tonight to put... to put——' She stopped abruptly, suddenly realising what she'd been about to do. How could she tell the truth and save herself, yet implicate Kenny? She fell silent, and saw his eyes narrow thoughtfully as he studied her. She'd seen pictures of him in the local papers over the years, but none of them had prepared her for the sheer impact of the man in the flesh. Just for a moment she let her eyes linger on the broad, high cheekbones, the fine, patrician nose, the well-shaped mouth.

How old was he, thirty-something? It was hard to tell because despite the experience stamped on his face there was no trace of silver in the black hair, which was swept back from his broad brow, and no apparent softening of the muscular frame. At a little under six feet tall, he looked superbly fit, the heavy black overcoat he was wearing emphasising the width of his shoulders, the narrow trimness of waist and hips. A man in the prime of life, in fact.

The judgement flashed into her mind like summer lightning, and abruptly she brushed it aside. She was just wasting time standing here. If she couldn't talk herself out of this mess, then she would have to find some way of escaping. She glanced almost casually round the room, looking for a way out, but apart from the door she'd come in by there was no other exit. Was it possible that she could push past Lang and make a run for it? With the advantage of surprise on her side, she might just do it.

'Try it if you feel lucky, lady. It would be my pleasure to stop you, believe me!'

How had he read her mind so easily? She didn't know, but she glared at him, hating him for his perception. 'I don't know what you mean.'

'Don't you? Maybe not. After all, even *thinking* about making a run for it would be stupid, and you're far from that or you wouldn't have got in here tonight, would you, Miss...?'

He paused, obviously expecting her to offer her name, but Alex snapped her lips together like a gin-trap. There was no way she was telling him her name, no way she was telling him anything! He could forget the old name, rank and serial number routine, because this little prisoner wasn't going to utter a word, and especially not one which would link her with Kenny!

'So you prefer to remain anonymous. I wonder why? I'm sure you will have to tell me sooner or later. But let's not worry about it too much right now. It will give us something to think about over the next few days, the intriguing puzzle of your identity.'

Alex frowned, shooting him a questioning glance from under her lashes. 'I don't think our involvement will run into days.'

'Oh, I disagree. It would be a shame to part too soon. You and I are destined to get to know one another much, much better, Jane.'

'My name isn't Jane,' she snapped, feeling a *frisson* of unease dance its way down her spine at the curious statement.

'Probably not, but in the absence of any other it will have to do.' He smiled thinly, his eyes narrowed as they slid over her set face. 'Jane Doe rather suits you, I think.'

Alex sniffed her disapproval, refusing to let him see how much he'd unnerved her as she walked round the desk to confront him boldly.

'This is getting us nowhere. I want to know what you intend to do. Are you going to carry on with all this nonsense, or are you going to let me leave? There is nothing missing. You can check for yourself, of course, but I didn't come here tonight to steal.'

'Perhaps there is nothing tangible missing, nothing you can pick up and put in your pocket, but what about what's inside here?' He leaned forwards and ran a finger across her brow. Alex shivered at the cool touch of his hand against her flesh, feeling her heart jolt then start to beat in a crazy little rhythm. She drew back abruptly, fighting against the urge to touch a finger to her brow, which seemed to be burning with a cold fire. It was just nerves, that was all, just this fine nervous tension which made it seem as if that light touch still lingered, leaving an imprint on her skin; yet her voice was strangely husky when she spoke.

'I don't know what you mean.'

'It's simple. I saw you reading the blueprints when I came into the office. You had them spread out on the floor while you studied them. What were you doing, memorising the modifications we have made to the engine so that you can go back and report to whoever you're working for?'

'No one sent me here for that! Don't be ridiculous. I know nothing at all about engines, so how on earth could I memorise what's on those plans? It's all double Dutch to me!'

'Is it? But I only have your word on that, Jane, and why should I take your word for anything when so far you've not even tried to give me any sort of an explanation for why you are here? I know what I saw when I came into this room, and I saw you reading those plans!'

'I wasn't! It's the truth.' There was desperation in her voice as she tried to convince him, but it was obvious that it had no effect on his judgement.

'So vehement in your denials, Jane. It would be tempting to believe you when you're such a good actress, but I know what I saw. Our competitors will go to any lengths to find out what changes we've made to the design. Sending you here is just another example of that.'

'But I know nothing about engines. Nothing! The blueprints had fallen on to the floor, and I was just trying to roll them back together. I wasn't reading them. There would be no point when I wouldn't understand a word!'

He *had* to believe her, yet looking at him Alex knew with a feeling of cold certainty that he didn't believe a single word she'd said. She fell silent, dreading the moment when he would call the police, as he surely would soon. The shame of that, of being handed over and charged like a common criminal! She would never be able to hold her head up in town again. Tears welled into her eyes at the thought, and she brushed them away with shaking fingers, biting her lip to hold back the sobs which racked her body.

'Don't waste your time trying that routine, lady. Tears don't cut any ice with me!'

Lang's voice was as scornful as his expression as he watched the tears coursing down her cheeks, and Alex stiffened, hating him then more than she had hated anyone. How dared he accuse her of faking tears? She would rather die before she stooped to those tactics in front of him. From all she'd heard and seen of Jordan Lang, he wouldn't know the meaning of compassion.

She glared at him, wiping the glittering traces of moisture off her face. 'Don't flatter yourself. I wouldn't credit you with enough sensitivity to bother wasting my time like that.'

'I'm pleased to hear it. It should make life simpler for both of us over the next few days if you cut out the helpless little female routine. We both know you're far from that, or you wouldn't have got this far tonight!' He glanced round, his mouth tightening into an unpleasant line as his eyes stopped on the blueprints still lying on the floor. He picked them up, his long fingers running up and down the smooth paper as he rolled them into a tight tube before laying them almost lovingly on the desk, and Alex found her eyes drawn to his hands, watching the way they caressed the paper back into shape.

'Yes, take a good look, Jane, a really good one, because that's the last you or anyone else outside this building is going to get of them until the engine is unveiled next week.'

There was something in his voice, something which made the skin on the back of Alex's neck start to prickle. She looked up, meeting the cold depths of his grey eyes, which now burned with an intensity that frightened her more than anything that had happened so far. Kenny had said that Lang would go to any lengths to protect the plans, and now she knew he hadn't been wrong in his assessment.

'What a good job I came back here tonight. I hadn't been planning on it. It was just an impulse that brought me here and spoiled your evening.

Another few minutes and you'd have got what you wanted, and no one would have been any the wiser, would they? Still, that's the luck of the draw; someone wins and someone loses. Now I think I'll lock these away from any more prying eyes.'

Pulling a bunch of keys out of his pocket, he unlocked the safe and stowed the plans inside. Alex watched him, wishing she could break this thrall of fear he seemed to have cast over her, but it seemed impossible to move a muscle. What was he going to do now...what? She wished she knew, yet, equally, dreaded finding out.

'Right, that's all sorted out, so I think we'd better be on our way.'

He slid a hand under her elbow to lead her to-wards the door, but all of a sudden Alex came to her senses and awoke from the trance. She dug in her heels, resisting him every step of the way so that he was forced to stop.

'Let me go! What are you doing? Where are you taking me?' She was panting with fear, the questions coming in little spurts, her face ashen, her eyes huge and terrified.

'Somewhere you won't be able to cause any more trouble for a few days.' He swung her round, his fingers biting into the soft flesh of her upper arms even through the heavy jacket as he held her in front of him. 'What did you expect? That I would let you go? Is that why they sent a woman, thinking I would treat her more softly?'

He laughed, a harsh, bitter sound which made Alex struggle even harder; but to no avail. The fingers gripping her didn't loosen, allowing her no chance to break free from the punishing grasp.

Desperate to make him let her go, she kicked out, and heard him grunt in pain as her toe connected heavily with his shin; but he still held on to her, his eyes glittering with fury as he shook her until she was too breathless to struggle further.

'Cut that out if you know what's good for you! I'm not letting you go with what you've got stored in that pretty little head!'

'Then call the police and hand me over to them.'

Minutes ago the idea had been frightening, but now it seemed like a ray of hope in a darkening world, and infinitely preferable to anything he had planned for her!

'And have your friends come and bail you out? Do you think I'm stupid, Jane? Sorry to disappoint you, but there is no way that is going to happen while things are at such a delicate stage. One hint that our competitors might have seen the designs for the prototype, and we'll have investors pulling their money out. No... the police are not going to hear about your visit to the factory tonight. No one is. It's going to be our little secret, yours and mine, something for us to share.' He glanced at his watch again, his mouth curling slightly as he caught her chin and forced her head up so that he could look directly into her eyes. 'Nine-thirty, Jane. It should have been midnight, really, I expect. Isn't that the customary time for strange things to happen? But I expect you'll remember this hour just as well in years to come.'

She snatched her head back away from the strangely unsettling touch of his fingers, feeling the tension uncurling like a snake in the pit of her stomach.

'What are you talking about?' she demanded, forcing a hard note to her voice, and praying he wouldn't see the shudder working its way through her body. 'You can't frighten me by making crazy statements.'

'Can't I? Maybe not. After all, you would have to be fairly tough to take on this job. In that case, then, I don't suppose it will bother you much if I tell you that as of nine-thirty tonight you no longer exist. You, Jane, are going to disappear off the face of the earth for the next seven days, and neither your friends nor whoever sent you here tonight are going to find you!'

Alex stared at him, too shocked to find a single word to say. It had to be a joke, surely? Yet, looking into his set face, she had the horrible feeling that it was no joke. He meant it, every single, terrifying word. Somehow, some way, Jordan Lang was going to make her disappear!

CHAPTER TWO

THE silence in the room must have lasted a full minute, the longest minute of Alex's life. She licked her dry lips, her eyes huge as she stared at Jordan Lang, wondering what she could say to stop him carrying out this crazy plan.

'Look, I know you're angry, but don't you think you're being a bit...? Let me go! Let me go, you big bully!'

All thoughts of trying to talk sense into him fled abruptly as he started to haul her towards the door. Desperately she twisted round, lashing out with her free hand, then gasped in alarm when he suddenly stopped and hauled her round to pin her against his chest.

'No! Don't do——'

She got no further, the words dammed in her throat as he bent and covered her mouth with his in a bruising kiss which stole the breath from her body. Behind her she could hear the sound of the door being opened, and she renewed her efforts to break free so that she could call for help; but with his hand clamping her head in place it was impossible.

'What the...? Oh, sorry, Mr Lang. I...I didn't know it was you in here, sir.'

The security guard's voice was filled with embarrassment as he realised he had broken in on what must have appeared to be a touchingly intimate moment between his employer and a lady friend, and Alex felt a surge of red-hot fury race through her as she realised that Jordan Lang must have heard the man coming along the corridor, and acted accordingly! If this was an example of how fast his mind worked, then she was going to have her work cut out catching him off guard!

The door closed again, but Lang made no attempt to remove his mouth from hers until the sound of the man's footsteps had faded. Raising his head a fraction, he smiled down into Alex's furious face with a mockery that made her want to do something desperate...and to hell with the consequences! Twisting free, she wiped a hand across her mouth to erase the taste of the kiss, her eyes filled with loathing.

'How dare you——?' she began, then stopped abruptly when he caught hold of her again and shook her roughly.

'How dare I? Haven't you got that wrong? *I* am the injured party here, and don't you forget it! It's my factory you broke into tonight, my designs which you tried to steal, my business which you have put in jeopardy, so you can cut out all the righteous indignation, and get things into true perspective! Frankly, I think you should be thanking your lucky stars, lady, that a kiss is all you've had to suffer. You wouldn't have got off half so lightly if you'd been a man!'

There was no doubting that he meant every word, and Alex shuddered as a fleeting picture of what might have happened if he'd come back and found Kenny with the plans flashed into her mind. The thought held her silent as Lang hustled her from the room, and along the corridor to the fire-escape. Pushing the heavy outer door open, he led her to the top of the open steps, his fingers tightening on her arm as she hesitated, not liking the look of the stairway which spiralled down into the darkness.

'Get a move on. We haven't got all night to waste.'

He urged her on, a dangerous move when she was already so unsure. Her foot slipped on the first frost-slick tread, and for a heart-stopping moment she teetered on the verge of falling headlong before he hauled her upright again.

'Forget it! Don't even think about trying any of your little tricks. There will be no police, no ambulance, nothing—not even if you break every rotten bone in your body. There is no way I am letting you out of my sight...understand?'

Alex gasped at the unfairness of the accusation. Muttering darkly under her breath, she marched down the rest of the steps, then stood and glowered at him when she reached the safety of the ground; but he appeared totally unmoved.

'Another little puzzle, so it appears. And an answer, of sorts.'

'What puzzle? What are you talking about now?' She eased the collar of her jacket up round her ears, shivering slightly as the icy wind touched coldly against her heated skin.

'How you got into the factory. You didn't seem to enjoy coming down the fire-escape, so I can't in all honesty see that you found the courage to climb in through any of the upper windows.' He shot a speculative glance up the side of the building, then looked back at her. 'How did you manage to get in, then, Jane, when I pay out a small fortune on security?'

Did he really think she was going to tell him? She hadn't enjoyed coming down that fire-escape, as he'd so rightly guessed, but it hadn't shaken her *so* much that she was prepared to divulge something so crucial! She smiled sweetly at him, her voice soft and gentle as a summer's breeze. 'That's for me to know and you to find out, isn't it?'

Anger crossed his face as her words hit home, and she took a hurried step backwards, wondering if she'd been wise to push him with the blatant gibe, then knew she hadn't when he laughed, a harsh explosion of sound which made her stomach clench in apprehension.

'Do you know, I am almost starting to enjoy this, Jane? Starting to enjoy all these little puzzles you keep setting for me. First there was the question of your identity, and now the even more intriguing one of how you managed to bypass the security systems. Solving them should help pass the time nicely where we are going.'

'And where is that? I hate to be a kill-joy and spoil your fun, but don't you think this is all a bit far-fetched? How on earth do you intend to spirit me away for a whole week?' She forced herself to sound calmly confident, to swallow down the fear she could feel like a cold lump in her throat.

'I wouldn't say it was far-fetched. Not at all. But of course I have the advantage of knowing where we are going.'

'And where is that?'

He smiled, his teeth gleaming white against his tanned skin. 'Surely that's for me to know and you to find out, isn't it?' he said quietly, tossing her own words back at her. 'You wouldn't really expect me to divulge that kind of information, Jane.'

'Don't call me by that stupid name,' Alex snapped, her nerves tingling like over-stretched violin strings. It was just so much talk, that was all—a way to frighten her into telling him who had sent her to the factory. There was no way he could really spirit her away!

'Tell me what your real name is, and I'll happily use it.' He raised a questioning brow, but Alex looked away, no more prepared to tell him now than she had been earlier. Even now he was speculating on how she'd got into the factory, so how long would it be before he realised she must have had inside help? The longer she could guard the secret of her identity, the more time she would have to find a way out of this mess.

'Jane, Jane, why are you being so stubborn? You must know that I shall find out sooner or later. It's only a matter of time. But if that's the way you want to play it, then so be it. Now come along. We can't afford to waste any more time. We have a long drive ahead of us tonight.'

He took her arm and led her towards one of the rear loading yards, where she could see a car parked, its white paintwork gleaming in the yellow beams of one of the security lights. Alex dragged her feet, trying desperately to put off the moment when she must get into the car.

'Don't try anything silly, will you? I don't want to have to hurt you, but the fact that you're a woman won't stop me if you try running off. There is too much at stake here to worry about the niceties of civilised behaviour!'

'Civilised behaviour', indeed! He wouldn't understand even the rudiments of it! With a haughty sniff, Alex slid into the car, and sat staring through the windscreen while Jordan climbed in and started the engine. He flicked a glance sideways at her before turning the car and heading towards the main gates.

'Still think it was worth it, then?'

'Worth what?'

'Whatever you're being paid? Sure it's enough to make up for all this, or are you starting to feel sorry that you came?'

'Yes,' she snapped, turning slightly to fix him with a hot glare. Deliberately she whipped up her anger, using it to quell the cold shivers of fear she could feel trickling through her body. 'Yes, I'm sorry I came, but not for the reasons you imagine! But don't think you'll get away with this, Jordan Lang. This is kidnapping! You could get sent to prison for this. It's a major crime!'

His expression never wavered from one of cold indifference as he slid the car to a gentle halt at the junction of the drive and the road. 'I'm sure it is. Interesting, isn't it? Which carries the stiffer penalty, kidnapping or industrial espionage? Seems to me that we're well matched, Jane. We both obviously have criminal leanings.'

'Speak for yourself! I have never done anything criminal in my life!'

'And what do you call tonight's little escapade?' he shot back, his mouth tightening when he saw the self-righteous expression on her face. 'You broke into my factory tonight, and if I hadn't come back would have made off with those plans!'

'I wasn't trying to steal them! I told you that before. Stop trying to whitewash what you're doing now by blaming me!'

'Who else is there to blame? Tell me, Jane. What were you doing there tonight if you weren't trying to steal?'

It was tempting, so tempting to put all this nightmare behind her. For one brief moment, Alex felt herself weakening before she came to her senses.

'I can't tell you.'

'Too damned right you can't! You can protest all you like, but there is no way you will ever convince me that I'm wrong!'

'I don't care what you think, Jordan Lang. You can go to hell for all I care!'

He laughed harshly, revving the engine as he swung the car out on to the road. 'I wouldn't be too hasty in my condemnations if I were you. Wherever I go, you go too. For the next seven days you and I are going to be as inseparable as lovers!'

Alex turned away, staring out of the window as she watched the lights from the factory fading into the distance, realising the utter futility of arguing with him any more. He would never believe her, not even if she told him the truth. He would think that she had made it up, that she and Kenny had been trying to steal the plans, not put them back. She would say nothing more, just bide her time and, at the first opportunity, get away from him. After all, he couldn't watch her day and night for seven whole days.

It sounded like the sensible thing to do but, as the car travelled on into the night, leaving the factory and Kenny further and further behind, Alex wasn't entirely convinced that being sensible would be enough...not when she was dealing with Jordan Lang!

Was this it, then? The place where he meant to hold her for the next week?

Rubbing the burning sting of exhaustion from her eyes, Alex peered through the windscreen, but there wasn't much to see apart from the sickly glow of light spilling from the cottage windows they were parked outside. Where were they? How far had they come? And, more importantly, what was going to happen now that they had arrived? She had no way of knowing, but the uncertainty if it all made her feel more afraid than ever.

'Stay here. And if you have any ideas about trying to run off, don't! You'll only regret it!'

Removing the keys from the ignition, Jordan climbed out of the car and strode towards the cottage. Alex watched him go, her eyes locked to his broad back as he knocked on the door, trying to stifle the mounting panic. She might only get this one chance, and she couldn't afford to miss it by panicking. Cautiously she unsnapped the seatbelt, then froze when he shot a quick look over his shoulder just as the door was opened, sending a flood of light spilling over the path. For a moment he didn't move, then stepped inside the house, and Alex swallowed down a half-choked sob of relief.

Flinging the car door open, she scrambled out, flinching as a cold flurry of rain pelted into her face. Steeling herself against the onslaught, she looked round to get her bearings, but it was impossible to decide which way to go when everywhere looked so darkly unfamiliar. Anxious not to waste any more valuable time, she chose a direction at random, and started forwards, then had to grab hold of the car roof when her feet slid wildly on the muddy surface.

'I thought I told you not to try anything silly, like running off.'

The voice came from behind her, and Alex gasped and spun round, then had to clutch hold of the car again as her feet lost their purchase on the ground once more. Helplessly, she watched as a dark figure loomed towards her, pressing closer to the car as Jordan Lang came and stopped in front of her— so close that she could feel the brush of his body against her own. Rain had flattened his dark hair to his skull and settled a layer of moisture over the hard planes of his face, so that he looked even more forbidding than ever, and Alex had to force herself to meet his eyes with an outward show of defiance.

'So you did, but surely you didn't expect me to follow orders, did you? That really was rather naïve of you.'

'So instead you decide to go running off into the open dressed like that?' He swept a hard look over her tight jeans and leather jacket. 'We're not in the middle of town now, sweetheart. You wouldn't last a couple of hours out on the hills in that outfit, delightful though it may be.'

'Your concern is touching,' she said, forcing a bite to her voice to hide the tremor she could feel inching its way through her body, as she felt his eyes running up the slender length of her legs in the tight jeans which were now clinging damply to every shapely curve. She moved self-consciously, then froze as her thigh brushed against the hardness of his, sending a shaft of awareness shooting through her.

'My concern isn't for you. It's for me. Frankly, I don't give a damn what happens to you, but, if you go running off, then I will be morally obliged to go after you! Now come along. Let's get a move on.'

He grasped her elbow and, after one swift abortive attempt to shake his hand off, Alex let it remain where is was rather than suffer the indignity of a tussle. She was still smarting from what he'd said and, if she was honest, still thrown off balance by that strange flash of physical awareness she'd experienced. What on earth was the matter with her? She must be more strung up by the night's events than she'd realised.

In total silence she let him lead her over the rough ground, then felt a jolt of surprise when he by-passed the cottage and carried on into the gloom of the night. If the cottage wasn't their destination, then where exactly were they going? She racked her brain, then felt her breath catch as a new and far more alarming destination sprang to mind. All of a sudden all the dreadful horror stories she'd ever read in the papers about kidnap victims being held in caves or underground passages came rushing back, and she moaned in dismay. The idea was totally uncivilised, but there again she already knew that Jordan Lang wasn't a civilised man!

Hearing the sudden whisper of sound, he shot a curious look sideways at her, his hand tightening round her arm.

'What's the matter?'

'Nothing. Why should there be anything the matter? I mean, why should any woman in her right mind be worried about being abducted in the middle of the night?'

He stopped abruptly, so abruptly that Alex cannoned into him as her feet skidded on the slippery grass.

'You've only got yourself to blame. You should have thought of the consequences before you broke into the factory tonight. Frankly, I'm not enjoying this any more than you are.'

'Aren't you? I beg to differ, Mr Lang. I'd say that you are getting quite a kick out of terrifying me like this! There's a name for people like you...sadist! That's exactly what you are—a sadist...Ohhh!'

The words dried in her throat as he swung her round in front of him, gripping her by the shoulders while he glared down into her startled face.

'Who the hell are you to be calling me names? You're nothing but a common thief, lady, and don't you forget it! If there's any name-calling to be done, then it's I who shall be doing it, do you hear?'

He set off again, dragging her with him so that Alex had to run to keep up with him; but she refused to ask him to slow down, refused to beg. She hated him to the very depths of her soul, and she would rather die first than ask him a favour!

Now that they had left the cottage behind, darkness once more enclosed them, making Alex wonder how he could see well enough to keep such a sure footing on the rough ground. It was only the punishing grip he maintained on her arm which kept her upright.

'Over there. To your right.'

With scant ceremony, Jordan hustled her along in front of him across a lumpy stretch of grass which oozed with mud. Alex scanned the darkness, but could see little through the driving rain until the dark shape of a building suddenly appeared in front of them. She stopped dead, ignoring Jordan's rough curse when he almost fell over her, her eyes locked to the building in sudden dread.

All right, so it wasn't a cave or underground passage, or any other of the places her imagination had conjured up, but, frankly, no one this side of Transylvania could call the rough-hewn building inviting. A couple of circling bats, a few blood-thirsty screams, and Dracula himself would have the ideal country retreat. But if Jordan Lang thought he could lock her up in there, then he was wrong!

She spun round, taking him by surprise as she wrenched her arm free and shoved him roughly aside. Then she was off, skidding her way across the grass towards the path. Behind her she could hear Lang's roar of anger, but she closed her mind to the sound, and concentrated on setting as much distance as she could between them. If she could only get back to the car and lock herself inside, then he would have one heck of a time getting her out again!

The jolt of some unseen restraint catching her round the knees brought her to the ground with a wind-stopping force. Alex lay still, wondering if she was dead, as a bone-crushing weight settled itself on her body, making it impossible to drag any air into her deflated lungs. Lights began to flash behind her eyes, making her head ache with their brilliance, so that it was almost a relief when everything started to go dark.

'Don't you dare pass out on me! Sit up, woman!'

The weight shifted, and she was hauled abruptly upright into a sitting position, but it was still impossible to breathe until something hit her a nasty wallop between the shoulder-blades. Her lungs whooshed open, and she coughed as she drew in great greedy gulps of the wet night air.

'Of all the crazy, irresponsible, stupid...'

The tirade ran on and on along such similar lines for several minutes and, despite herself, Alex was impressed by his repertoire of adjectives. She'd swear he never repeated himself even once! Slowly, she opened her eyes and looked at him, then felt the quite ridiculous urge to giggle. She swallowed hard, trying desperately to force it down and remember that this was not a laughing matter, but, as her vision improved and she got an even better look at Jordan Lang, it became impossible.

From head to toe he was covered in mud, his black hair plastered with it, his face spattered, his expensive overcoat sleek as a seal's under its sticky wet coating. He looked so different now from the suave picture of well-tailored elegance he'd presented in the office that Alex felt the giggle turn into a full-blown laugh.

'So you think it's funny, do you?' he ground out, his eyes gleaming in a way which made the laughter bubble and suddenly die in her throat almost as quickly as it had begun. Alex pushed her matted hair out of her eyes, and looked warily at him, her eyes huge and getting huger as she saw the dawning expression on his face—saw and correctly interpreted its meaning! With a shrill cry of alarm, she tried to scramble to her feet, but he caught her ankle and hauled her back down to the ground.

'Oh, no, you don't! You're not getting away from me again. You've had your fun, and now I think it's my turn!'

He pulled her to him and bent his head, taking her mouth in an angry kiss meant to punish. Alex twisted and turned, fighting to free her lips from the rough assault, but she was no match for his strength. He raised his hand, twisting his fingers into the damp length of her hair, pulling her head back so that she gasped in pain as the tender roots of her hair were dragged sharply. His tongue slid into her part-open mouth as he used the moment to deepen the kiss, tangling with hers, its movements deliberately provocative as he sought to force her to respond. Alex tried to avoid the hot, probing intimacy of the kiss, tried to avoid the sensuous stroking of his tongue against hers, but he was quite relentless as he held her head in place and continued kissing her until she was breathless and shaking, a fine tremor coursing through each fibre of her body.

Just for a moment, for a tiny second out of time, she succumbed to the tantalising caress, and kissed him back; then, with a low moan of anguish, she realised what she was doing. She dragged her mouth free, rubbing her hand over her lips time and again, but nothing could erase the lingering taste and feeling of heat imprinted on her skin. Tears of anger and shame sprang to her eyes, and she brushed them away, looking up at Jordan through misty lashes. He was watching her, his eyes shadowed, gleaming a flat silver as he stared intently at her; and for some strange reason Alex found she couldn't look away.

'Hey, there! Are you all right, Mr Lang? What's happened?'

The shout came from the direction of the cottage, and Alex jumped in surprise, swinging round towards it. A man was standing on the step, holding a lamp above his head as he peered out at them. He took a hesitant step forwards, and Jordan swore softly as he scrambled to his feet, pulling Alex up with him.

'Everything is fine, Owen. Nothing to worry about. You go on back inside. Leave the car until morning. There's no point in you getting a soaking.'

The man raised a hand in acknowledgement, then went in and closed the door. Alex shivered as the light was abruptly cut off, leaving her and Jordan in almost total darkness, and she wished she'd had the presence of mind to shout for help before the man had disappeared. Still, one good thing to come out of it all was that she now had a fair idea where they were, thanks to hearing Owen's lilting accent: Wales. Though her heart sank as she realised just how far they'd come.

'Come along. We've wasted enough time here.'

Jordan caught hold of her arm, and attempted to steer her back up the path, but there was no way she was going back up there again!

'No!' she shouted defiantly, pulling back like a reluctant puppy on the end of its lead.

'No? I don't think you are really in any position to refuse, do you?' His gaze dropped to her mouth, and Alex felt heat rush through her at the silent reminder of the kiss he'd forced upon her; but she refused to be beaten into compliance. There was no way he was taking her back up that hillside and locking her away in that dreadful place!

'I will *not* go back up there and let you lock me up in that... that barn!'

'Lock you up? Is that what this is all about? My God, woman, what kind of a man do you take me for?' Anger flashed across his face as he hauled her round in front of him, jerking her back when she tried to pull herself away.

'Frankly, lady, you deserve to be locked up in there for the next ten years for what you've done tonight; but for your information that wasn't what I intended to do, tempting though the idea is.'

'Then what do you intend? Why are you leaving the car here? It's hardly the sort of night for a pleasant stroll!'

'Because there is no way I can take it any further up these tracks without ruining its suspension. I keep a jeep in that barn. We'll have to use that now to get the rest of the way up the mountain.'

'Oh.'

'"Oh", indeed.' He glared down at her, his eyes narrowed as he studied her pale face, and Alex shivered at the cold anger in their depths. 'Another one, then, Jane?'

'Another what?' Her voice was low, a faint murmur of sound nearly swallowed up by the whine

of the wind; but he caught it, and smiled thinly,
little amusement on his face.

'Another puzzle, of course.' He laughed, a grim
sound which lingered on the rough night air like
something tangible. 'I wonder who it was who gave
me such bad press that you believed I would happily
lock you away in a deserted building? Whoever
you're involved with is definitely not a member of
the Jordan Lang fan club!'

Without another word he took her arm and led
her back up the track, his face set into grim lines
of anger. Alex stole a quick glance at his stern
profile, then looked hurriedly away, wondering if
there wasn't just the tiniest grain of truth in what
he'd said. If Kenny hadn't implanted that idea
about Jordan Lang's lack of civility into her mind,
then would she really have jumped to such a hasty
conclusion, and accused him of planning such a
terrible deed?

She didn't know, but the idea that she might have
misjudged him made her feel strangely uneasy. She
wanted to see Jordan as the bad guy, now more
than ever, because she had the feeling that to see
him in any other light could be asking for more
trouble than she could handle!

CHAPTER THREE

BY THE time they reached their destination, Alex was a wreck. It had taken them a good hour more of driving, an hour spent clutching hold of the edge of the seat while Jordan negotiated the jeep round a series of heart-stopping bends. In the dark, Alex had gleaned only an indistinct glimpse of how the mountain fell away into a steep drop, but that had been enough! She'd spent the rest of the journey with her eyes closed, praying that Jordan's nerves were made of sterner stuff than hers. A couple of careless inches to the left, a slight misjudgement at the next hairpin bend and... She closed her mind to what might follow, cursing Kenny to hell and back for putting her through such an ordeal!

'We're here.'

Jordan cut the engine and set the handbrake, and slowly Alex opened her eyes, breathing a quiet sigh of relief when she saw there wasn't a cliff-edge or hairpin bend in sight, just the comforting bulk of a small house, looking invitingly solid in the glow of the headlamps. For a thankful moment she let her eyes linger on the welcome sight, then looked further afield, but there were no other houses to be seen. Obviously the place was as isolated as Jordan Lang had said it would be, and a tiny cold flurry of fear started to inch its way down her spine.

'Stay here while I go and open up and get some lamps lit.'

He jumped out of the jeep and disappeared inside the house, leaving Alex staring after him in something akin to panic. Now that they had finally arrived, the true precariousness of her situation hit her, making her realise just how vulnerable she was going to be, alone in the house with him. Desperate to find some way out, she looked frantically round, and caught sight of the keys dangling from the ignition. He was taking a chance leaving the keys behind, wasn't he? What was to stop her from taking the jeep and driving off?

It was a tantalising thought, and for thirty delicious seconds she savoured it greedily, wondering if all her prayers had been answered, before coming to her senses with a deflated bump. There was no way she could take the jeep and drive it down that treacherous track in the darkness. It would be suicidal even to attempt it, and Jordan Lang knew it!

In a real fit of temper she jumped out of the jeep and strode into the house, yelping as she banged her shin painfully against some unseen object. Hopping on one leg, she rubbed the bruised flesh, ignoring Jordan when he came into the hall with a lamp to see what all the commotion was about.

'I thought I told you to wait in the jeep. Can't you ever do a thing you're told to?'

Alex ignored the sarcasm just as easily as she'd ignored his previous, and obviously sound advice. Gingerly she set her foot down, and shot a quick look round but, frankly, she was in no mood to appreciate the cosiness of the lamplit hall with its pale grey walls and red rugs scattered across the grey flagstoned floor.

'And what exactly do you intend to do with me now that we're here?' She flashed him a tight smile, her expression one of cool mockery which belied her true feelings, the anxiety she could still feel gnawing at the pit of her stomach. There was no way she was going to let him know how afraid she felt.

'Come along, then, Mr Lang. I'm just dying to hear what's in store for me. Is there a nice cosy little cellar somewhere, or do you intend to keep me bound and gagged for the next week?'

'What a very active imagination you have. You're wasting your time being a thief. You should be writing for television with a mind like yours.'

'I am *not* a thief!'

'Oh, spare me... please. I've heard your claims to virtue so many times tonight that they're starting to get boring.'

'That's because it's true. I didn't go to the factory to steal your rotten blueprints!'

'Of course you didn't. You just happened to wander in there, find your way up to the office, and there they were, lying about with a little note on them saying "Read me". Forgive me if I find it hard to believe!'

'Oh, very amusing. But I'm still waiting to hear what little treat you have in store for me.' Alex strode along the hall, and glanced into one of the downstairs rooms, then shot a quick look over her shoulder. 'I can't see any signs of racks or thumb-screws, but I'm sure a man like you won't have overlooked the necessities, not when you are obviously so adept at abducting people.'

'I wonder what sort of people you usually associate with. No, I hate to disappoint you, but there are no racks, no thumbscrews, not even a nice damp cellar. The best I can offer you is bed.'

'What?' Her voice rose an octave, echoing shrilly round the hall, and she saw him wince, but she didn't care as every single one of her fledgeling fears sprouted wings and fluttered wildly inside her. If he thought for one moment that she would . . . that he could . . .

'What on earth is wrong with you now?'

He moved towards her, holding the lamp aloft as he stared down at her white face, and Alex took a hasty step backwards, balling her hands into fists.

'Don't you come any closer,' she warned. 'Or I'll . . .'

'You'll what? Scream the place down? Be my guest, but I warn you that you'd just be wasting your breath. There's no one for miles around; no one to hear if you stood on the roof and screamed until you were blue in the face.' He smiled, a faint gleam in his eyes now as he set the lamp down and took a few more slow steps towards her. 'Getting cold feet, are you, Jane? Suddenly realising just what you've got yourself into?'

He reached out so swiftly that she had no chance to avoid him as he slid a hand round the back of her neck and pulled her to him. Cupping her chin with his other hand, he tilted her face to stare down into her frightened eyes. 'Does the idea of us being here all alone bother you, Jane?'

'No! No, of course it doesn't bother me. You can't frighten me, Jordan Lang!'

'No? Then why is your pulse racing?' He laid a long finger against the tiny pulse which was beating a frantic tattoo at the base of her neck, stroking it delicately over the soft skin. 'If it's not fear, then what is it? Desire?'

'No!' With a quick twist of her body, she broke free, and backed away from him. 'All right, so I am afraid; who wouldn't be in my position? You've brought me here to this god-forsaken spot, and how do I know what you intend to do next?'

He shrugged, but made no move to follow her, standing relaxed and seemingly at ease in the pool of light cast by the lamp. 'You don't. You're at my mercy now. I can do anything I like with you, can't I? And no one... no one will be any the wiser.'

His voice was low, even, as though he were discussing the price of shares, the weekly shopping—anything but her fate; and Alex had to hold herself rigid to stem the mounting tide of fear.

'You're mad, do you know that? Mad if you think you can get away with this.'

'And who is going to stop me? I really can't see whoever sent you to the factory tonight coming forwards and asking questions about your whereabouts!'

'You're wrong. My b——' She stopped dead, the word freezing on her lips as she suddenly realised what she'd been about to say. Jordan was watching her intently, a cold expression on his face, and in a sudden flash Alex realised that he had been deliberately goading her, hoping to rattle her so that she would let something slip. How nearly he'd succeeded!

She drew in a shaky little breath, feeling her legs trembling in reaction. 'It won't work. I won't tell you anything more than I've told you already.'

'We'll see. It's early days yet. A week's a long time, and I have the feeling that you might change your mind before that time is up.'

'Never,' she said hotly. 'Never!'

'Never is an even longer time, but I admire your loyalty even if it is sadly misplaced.' He straightened, picking up the lamp so that its rays fell directly on to his face, setting the bones into stark relief, making his features look even harsher. 'Now I think it's time for bed. Maybe things will look different to you in the morning, once you've had time to think everything through.'

He started towards the stairs, but Alex held back, still beset by her earlier fears. He glanced back at her, his eyes lingering on her pale face, the rigid tension in her slim body. 'Well, aren't you coming?'

'Look, if you think that I'm going to...to...' She couldn't bring herself to say the words aloud, colour ebbing and flowing in her face as she met his knowing gaze and saw the mocking smile which curved his lips.

'To sleep with me? Is that what you're finding so difficult to say? Ah, Jane, life is full of disappointments for you today, especially when you seem so intent on casting me as the villain. No, for your information I have no intention of carrying you off to my bed and having my wicked way with you, tempting though the idea is. I prefer my women to have less criminal tendencies than you exhibit!

'Now, if you'll follow me, I'll show you which room you can use. Oh, and just one more thing...don't think for one minute that you can run off from here. Quite apart from the fact that the house is miles from anywhere, I have no intention of letting you out of my sight until the prototype is unveiled.' He swept a look over her, his face so hard that she quailed inwardly. 'There is too much sunk into this project to let you or anyone else ruin it. No matter what it takes, Jane, I intend to safeguard the project!'

He turned away and walked up the stairs and, after a momentary hesitation, Alex followed him. Every instinct was screaming at her to run, to get as far away from him and this house as she could, but she knew she couldn't risk attempting it at present. There was no doubt in her mind that he'd meant what he'd said, that he would do whatever necessary to protect his precious engine. But somehow, some way, she had to find a way out of here even if it meant lulling him into a false sense of security so that he would be off his guard. The one thing she couldn't do was spend the next week here with him!

Alex couldn't sleep, not with everything that had happened, and everything that was to come. Tossing back the blankets, she climbed out of bed, and crossed to the window to look out. It was still raining, a heavy driving rain which slanted across the hillside and sent huge drops scurrying down the window-pane. A faint moon had risen, and she could just make out the stark outline of the trees, their bare branches twisting under the force of the wind. It was a bleak outlook, and after a few minutes she turned away, looking round the room—

for what? Inspiration? Reassurance? Whatever it was, she didn't find it in the small room.

With a weary sigh she walked back to the bed, then stopped, her eyes lingering on the rumpled covers with a hint of distaste. She didn't want to get back into that bed and make another pretence at sleeping, with her mind whirling in smaller and smaller circles as she searched for a way out of this whole mess. To hell with Jordan Lang! She was going downstairs, and he could either like it or lump it!

She ran down the stairs, her bare feet making no sound on the thick carpet, then stopped at the bottom, her eyes going longingly to the door. It would be so easy to open that door and walk out—the solution to all her problems. So what was stopping her from doing it? The fact that Lang had told her the house was isolated? For all she knew he could have been lying, tricking her as he had so nearly tricked her before. She would be a fool to miss such a golden opportunity by being gullible!

She took an eager step forwards, then stopped dead when a deep voice spoke almost directly behind her.

'I wouldn't do that if I were you.'

Heart pounding, she spun around, her eyes huge as she spotted him lounging in a doorway, watching her with an expression on his face which was frankly scary. Slowly, he slid an assessing look over her body, then looked back at her face, his eyes flat and devoid of feeling so that she felt chilled to the bone.

'You disappoint me, Jane. I expected more from you than an attempt to leave via the front door, and in that state of undress. Unless, of course, you hoped it might distract me.' He trailed another insulting glance up the length of her legs, his lips curling in derision. 'Nice, but I think I'll pass this time, thank you.'

How dared he? Did he honestly believe that she had deliberately come downstairs dressed like this to... to distract him? She swept a glance down the bare length of her slender legs showing under the thigh-length hem of her shirt, and felt the colour rise in her cheeks as she realised for the first time exactly how revealing her outfit was.

She'd removed the wet jeans and jacket to go to bed, choosing to sleep only in the thick shirt and panties, and she had never paused to consider how she looked before rushing downstairs. Now she could feel the embarrassment curling hotly inside her as she realised what a picture she presented to the man who was watching her. She took a hasty step towards the staircase, anxious to get back to the bedroom and away from that coldly assessing scrutiny, then yelped in pain as her bare toe grazed against a sharp corner of one of the flags. Blood started to ooze from the cut, welling quickly into a small pool, dark red against the grey stone floor, and she swallowed hard, feeling suddenly queasy at the sight of it.

'Damnation, woman! Look what you're doing!' With a low growl of annoyance, Jordan stepped forwards and swept her up over his shoulder, striding towards the rear of the house along the hall before Alex had a chance to realise what was happening.

'Put me down!' she ordered, then repeated it a shade more forcefully when he took no notice. 'Put...me...down! What do you think you're doing?' She beat her fists against his shoulders in a tattoo, marking time with her instructions, then stopped abruptly when he turned his head and glared straight into her eyes.

'Stop that now! You've caused quite enough trouble for one night, and I have no intention of letting you bleed all over the floor and ruin it just to round things off!'

Well, she hadn't expected a show of concern or even a hint of contrition that she had injured her foot on his rotten flags, but that was carrying insensitivity too far even for him! Mouthing insults as to his pedigree under her breath, Alex was forced to suffer the indignity of having him carry her like some sort of lumpy package before he deposited her none too gently on one of the kitchen chairs.

'Thank you. You are so kind,' she said sarcastically, trying to ease the shirt-tail down over her bare thighs, yet not let him see that she was at all conscious of her semi-nudity. 'You really have missed your vocation. With your obvious concern for the welfare of your fellow man, you should have been a missionary. I can just picture you doing good deeds, helping the injured with that particular brand of charm you display—ow, that hurts!'

She grasped her foot, cradling it gently as she studied the dark stain from the liquid he'd swabbed round the cut.

'Iodine,' he said succinctly, catching hold of her ankle to pull her foot back and take another swipe with the iodine-soaked cotton wool. 'There's no point in taking a chance on it becoming infected. I'm sure you're brave enough to put up with a little discomfort, with your background and training.'

'What do you mean, my background?' she snapped, rubbing a few drops of moisture out of her eyes. 'You know nothing about my background!'

'Maybe not, but I just had a vague idea that anyone who earns her living from industrial espionage would have to be tough. It isn't a job for the faint-hearted.'

'I keep telling you, I am not a spy! Why won't you listen to me?'

'Oh, I'm listening all right. It's just the believing I find difficult. Now stay there while I get a plaster to put on that cut.'

Resting her foot on the seat of one of the chairs, Jordan walked over to the cupboards, opening one to sort through the contents. Alex glowered at his broad back, her eyes shooting sparks of annoyance. Why wouldn't he even *try* to believe her? Why did he have to be so all-fired certain that she was guilty?

'I'm sure there's a box somewhere in here.' He stretched up to skim a searching hand along the top shelf, the muscles in his back rippling with the movement. He obviously kept a change of clothes at the house, because he'd discarded the suit he'd been wearing before and changed into slim-fitting denim jeans, which clung lovingly to his long legs and narrow hips. With them he wore a deep blue sweatshirt, and Alex felt her mouth go suddenly dry as it rose up when he stretched, giving tantalising glimpses of smooth brown flesh. Hurriedly she averted her gaze, then nearly jumped out of her skin when he appeared in front of her with a plaster in his hands.

'Here you are. I knew I had some somewhere.' He stripped the backing off the piece of tape and pressed it over the wound, his long fingers cool as they brushed against her bare toes. 'Right, that should do it, but you'd be well advised to get dressed before you start wandering round in here next time. It will save any further accidents.' He skimmed a look up the bare length of her legs, and Alex felt the colour flood to her face as she felt the touch of those grey eyes as if it were something tangible. She stood up abruptly, almost toppling over her chair in her haste to get away, aware that he was watching her with an intent scrutiny, which made her feel more self-conscious than ever. What on earth was the matter with her? She was acting more like some shy little schoolgirl rather than a mature woman who had experienced her fair share of male attention! Annoyed with herself, she rushed into speech.

'Thank you. I'll be more care——' She stopped abruptly as the lights went out, plunging the room into darkness.

'Damnation! The generator must have broken down. I thought it didn't look too good when I started it up before. Stay there while I get a lamp in here.'

He left the room, returning in the space of seconds with an oil lamp, and set it down on the table, fixing Alex with a hard stare as he lifted a jacket off the peg behind the door.

'You'd better stay in here while I see what I can do with it. I don't want you wandering round the place and causing more damage. Oh, and, if you have any more bright ideas about running away, then forget them, or I might just do something we'll both regret!'

Alex stiffened at the undisguised threat, hating him at that moment more than ever. 'Don't worry, I'm not a fool!'

'I'm glad to hear it.'

He walked out, closing the door quickly behind him as a blast of wind and rain flurried into the kitchen. Alex sat down again at the table, hugging her arms tightly round her body, but it did little to stem the cold chills. Jordan Lang was her enemy, and she'd been a fool to forget that even for a moment. Never again would she let herself experience that crazy flurry of attraction she'd felt before!

Where on earth was he?

Pushing the curtain aside, Alex stared out of the window, but there was still no sign of Jordan returning. He'd been gone almost an hour now, yet surely it shouldn't take so long to get the generator working again? Letting the curtain fall, she looked round the kitchen, rubbing one bare foot against the other in an attempt to warm them up. With the generator out of action the house had grown distinctly chilly, and she could feel goose-bumps rising on every exposed inch of flesh. Whether she was flouting his orders or not, she would have to go upstairs and get dressed or she would catch pneumonia.

Holding the lamp carefully in front of her, Alex made her way through the dark house, feeling easier once she was back in the bedroom. There was something unnerving about being in the strange house alone, hearing all the unfamiliar sounds of the wind whistling through the eaves. She was sorely tempted to climb back into bed and pull the covers over her head as she'd done as a child, but some niggling little feeling wouldn't let her. There was something *odd* about Jordan's staying outside such a long time, and leaving her alone!

Dragging on her clothes, she hurried downstairs again and opened the kitchen door to peer out into the darkness.

'Jordan! Where are you?'

The wind caught her shouts and carried them away, but she could hear no answering cries, and the feeling that there was something wrong intensified. With a sigh of resignation, she stepped outside, calling herself every kind of fool for worrying about a man who didn't care a jot about her; but there was no way she would be able to live with herself if anything had happened to him.

Rounding the corner of the house, she yelped in pain as a trailing bramble caught round her ankle, then followed it by a gasp when she caught sight of the figure lying on the ground. Fighting free of the prickly barbs, she ran across the grass and fell to her knees beside him. He was lying so completely still, his eyes closed, his dark hair sleeked back from his forehead with rain, and Alex felt her heart lurch with fear. Was he dead?

With trembling fingers, she reached out to touch the side of his face, them jumped violently when he moaned. With a fierce feeling of relief, she pressed her hand against the pulse beating in his neck, feeling the steady throbbing against her flesh. Heaven knew what had happened, but that really wasn't the issue right at that moment. It was far more important that she get him inside out of the storm.

He was heavy, far heavier than his lean build intimated, and, by the time Alex managed to drag him inside the house and get him on to the huge old-fashioned sofa in what was evidently the living-room, she was exhausted. Just for a moment she allowed herself the luxury of slumping against the end of the sofa, then forced herself to her feet. She might have got him inside out of the rain, but she couldn't leave him lying there in wet clothing, or he would catch his death, and that really would give her noisy conscience something to worry about!

Perspiration beaded her brow as she was forced to manhandle the full weight of his torso to get his jacket and sweatshirt off. Just for a moment her eyes lingered on the tanned width of his muscular chest with its light dusting of fine black hair, before determinedly she focused her attention lower and steeled herself to remove his sodden jeans. Slipping his shoes and socks off was easy enough, but when it came to actually unfastening the snap of the jeans she had to draw in a shaky little breath to steady her nerves. It was ridiculous to feel embarrassed when she was doing it solely for his own good, but Alex couldn't help the hot little spirals from curling through her as her fingers brushed against the hard muscles of his stomach when she pulled the metal clasp apart and slid the zipper down.

'What are you doing?'

She gasped in shock as his hand came out and caught her wrist, pressing her fingers more intimately against his body. Wide-eyed, she looked up at him, feeling her pulse skip a beat when she saw that his eyes were open and he was watching her.

'I asked what you were doing!' He spoke slowly, his lips moving with laborious concentration as though he found the effort almost too much, and instinctively she tried to soothe him.

'It's all right. Lie still; I'm just going to get your wet clothes off before you catch a chill.'

He stared at her for a long moment, obviously trying to make sense of what she was saying, his eyes hazy. Then slowly the haze began to clear, and he tried to sit up, falling back against the cushion with a groan of pain as he clutched his head.

'What the hell did you hit me with?'

Alex gasped then rushed into speech, anxious to disabuse him of that idea! 'Nothing! I mean, I didn't hit you...I didn't!'

'Then how did I get this lump on my head?'

He pulled her hand up to his head and pushed her fingers into the thick damp hair so that she could feel the huge lump distorting his scalp. Alex pulled away, trying to free her hand from his, but he wouldn't let her go.

'I didn't do that!' she repeated hoarsely. She struggled frantically, twisting her arm, then stilled when she saw the spasm of pain which crossed his face as she jarred his head. He closed his eyes again, his breathing short and laboured, his face turning the colour of putty under its tan.

'Are you all right? Jordan? Can you hear me? Jordan!'

There was a sharp anxiety in her voice as she leaned towards him, studying his ebbing colour, followed by intense relief when he opened his eyes again and looked at her in that familiarly mocking way.

'Such touching concern. Should I be flattered that you care so much about my welfare? Or is it more a case of you realising what you've done, and that you could have been adding manslaughter to all the other charges laid against you?'

Why, of all the nerve! After all she'd done, half killing herself dragging him in here! She should have left him out in that storm to rot! Exasperated by such pig-headed determination to see only the bad in anything she did and never the good, Alex glared at him, sorely tempted to give him a matching lump on the other side of his thick head.

'I did *not* hit you, though now I rather wish I had! You were lying unconscious on the ground when I found you.'

'And what were you doing out there? Making another attempt to escape, even after I'd warned you what I'd do to you?' He glowered at her, his grey eyes dark with anger, his mouth thinned into a mean line which made a little quiver rise in her stomach.

'No! I'd gone outside to see what was wrong. You were out there ages, and I was...' she hesitated, loath to admit her feelings to him, then carried on with a defiant toss of her head '...worried.'

'Worried? About me?' He laughed bitterly, then winced, resting his head back against the arm of the sofa. 'The only thing you were worried about,

Jane, was your own skin. What really happened? Did you creep up behind me and hit me on the head, meaning to make a run for it once I was out cold?'

'No!' She shouted the denial, but he ignored her, carrying on as though she had never spoken.

'And then what happened? Did you suddenly have second thoughts, and realise that leaving me out in that storm was tantamount to murder?'

'No! Why must you keep saying those horrible things? I didn't hit you!'

'Same as you didn't try to steal the blueprints. There are an awful lot of things you didn't do, Jane.'

There was a weary finality in his voice as he closed his eyes again, and Alex looked at him in concern, her anger suddenly forgotten. No matter how infuriating he could be, she had to remember that he was injured, though how badly she couldn't tell. He must have been unconscious for some time before she found him, so there was a strong possibility that he was suffering from concussion. What he needed was proper medical attention, and the only way to get that was by driving the jeep back down that track.

'I'm cold.'

Alex jumped when he suddenly spoke, her hand running automatically over his chest to test the coolness of his flesh with her fingers.

'Mmm, very nice, but I'm still cold.'

She snatched her hand away, feeling the colour flood into her face when she saw the glint of mockery in his grey eyes. She stood up abruptly and hurried to the door, not daring to look at him again as she murmured, 'I'll fetch a blanket for you.'

She ran up the stairs, stumbling over the top tread in the dark, wishing she'd thought to bring the lamp up out of the hall. As quickly as she could, she stripped a couple of blankets off her bed and bundled them up to take them downstairs, then paused, realising that she had to give herself time to think about what she should do. Everything had happened so fast since she'd found him lying outside, and she would do neither of them any favours by rushing headlong into the wrong course of action.

'Where the hell are you? Damn you, woman, if you're trying to run out on me, then I won't be responsible for my actions!'

Alex jumped as she heard the angry roar echoing up the stairs. Trailing the blankets, she hurried along the landing, and peered down into the dimly lit hall, gasping in dismay at the sight which met her eyes.

Jordan was standing in the open doorway, swaying perilously as he hung on to the doorframe. Even as she watched, he took an unsteady step into the hall, then staggered as his knees started to buckle. Dropping the blankets, Alex sprinted down the stairs, her blue eyes hot with anger as she looped his arm over her shoulders and half carried, half dragged him back into the room to push him back on to the sofa.

'Of all the stupid, irresponsible, foolhardy...' Now, when had she heard that before? The words dried up as she suddenly remembered where she'd heard a similar tirade, finally placing it down to when they had performed that little tussle in the mud a few hours earlier. Her mouth tightened, and she glared at him, now doubly furious both with his stupidity and with the fact that she was starting to sound like him! For her own peace of mind, if not his health, it was definitely time to end this alliance!

In angry silence she swung his legs up on to the sofa, then ran upstairs to fetch the blankets, tucking them round him with sharp, jerky little movements. Stepping back, she shot a quick glance round then marched towards the door.

'Where are you going?'

She flicked him a brief glance, one slender eyebrow raised in a mocking curve. 'I'll give you three guesses.'

'You're leaving?'

'Got it in one. Well done, Mr Lang. That blow on the head doesn't appear to have affected your reasoning at least.'

'To hell with my reasoning! You can't go and leave me here!' He half rose, trying to sit up, then groaned and fell back against the cushions. Alex steeled her heart to the pathetic picture he made lying there, the purpling bruise showing darkly against his temple, his dark hair all ruffled in a way that made her fingers itch to brush the silky strands back into place.

'I don't think you're in any position to stop me, do you?' she said, forcing a hard little note to her voice to hide the momentary softening. 'Anyway, if it's any consolation, I'm going to try and get some medical help for you, so you won't be on your own too long.'

'But I'll be alone until it arrives. Don't leave me here like this, Jane...please.'

He sounded so lost and helpless, his voice throbbing with something which tugged at her heart-strings, and Alex hesitated, wondering if it was wise to leave him on his own. What if he suffered a relapse? Or tried something silly like walking about again? Head injuries were tricky things, and there was no knowing what the next hour or so could bring.

Suddenly uncertain that going for help was the right thing to do, she opened her mouth to reassure him that she'd stay, then felt her temper rise in a sudden red-hot surge as she saw the expression on his handsome face. He was doing it deliberately. Quite intentionally playing on her emotions to keep her there!

'Why, you low-down, double-dealing, conniving——'

'Tut-tut, Jane, such language, and in front of an injured man as well!' He smiled suddenly, the first real smile she had ever seen him give, and just for one crazy moment she felt her heart flutter before she brought it back under control. She stormed out of the door and ran along the hall, her hand hovering on the door-lock as she heard him shout.

'I shall find you, Jane. Even if I have to move heaven and earth, I shall find you and make you pay for what you've done!'

There was no laughter in the deep voice now, no mockery, just a steely determination which made the blood rush to her head in fear. She wrenched the door open, slamming it behind her before racing over the grass to the jeep and starting the engine with a roar. Just for a second she glanced back at the house, then turned the vehicle in a slow circle and headed back down the path, trying to close her mind to those vengeful words which kept echoing round and round in her head.

There was nothing to worry about now. Once she had found help for Jordan Lang, then she could put this whole unsavoury incident behind her and get on with her life, safe in the knowledge that he had no idea who she was or why she'd been in the factory. There was no way he would ever find her. She'd make certain of that!

CHAPTER FOUR

IT WAS the waiting that was the worst. No matter how positive she tried to be, Alex woke up each morning wondering if today would be the day that Jordan Lang tracked her down. It didn't seem to matter how many times Kenny reassured her that they had got away with it; there was always that niggling little doubt at the back of her mind that somehow Jordan would find her. It was ridiculous, of course, because they didn't move in the same circles, and were unlikely to come into contact again; but she couldn't prevent the feeling of impending doom which seemed to hang like a great black cloud over her head.

In an effort to dispel the feeling, she spent more and more time working, almost doubling her output of handcrafted jewellery, to the delight of the London store which had been begging her for extra supplies for months. The subsequent increase in revenue came in very useful, enabling her to make an extra payment on the loan, so maybe the black cloud had a silver lining after all.

The days crept past, slid into weeks, and finally Alex started to relax a bit. There had never been any mention made of the incident in the factory, so maybe it had all been just a storm in a teacup which wouldn't blow up into a typhoon. Jordan Lang must have realised that he had been mistaken about her, and sensibly decided to let the matter drop.

Feeling more at ease, Alex locked the shop one day and hurried upstairs to the flat, surprised to find that Kenny was already home.

'You're early. What happened, did you get sent home early for good behaviour?' She shot him a laughing glance, then felt the smile freeze on her lips when she saw the expression on his face. All of a sudden that cloud was gathering again, pressing down on her head with its full weight of impending doom. It took every scrap of strength she possessed to ask the question she didn't want to ask.

'Has something happened about the blueprints?'

Her voice was hoarse with strain, and Kenny stood up and caught her by the shoulders, his hands gripping her painfully hard.

'I'm sorry, Lexie. I never should have got you into this.'

'What's done is done, Kenny, and all the wishing in the world won't change it. Just tell me what's happened now.'

She shook him off and walked to the window, rubbing her hands up and down her arms, but nothing seemed to stem the iciness that was stealing through her body. She should have known it was all going too smoothly. Jordan Lang wasn't the kind of man who would ever turn the other cheek.

'The whole factory was buzzing when I got in this morning. Seems there has been a leak about the new design, and Lang had given orders that he wanted to interview every person who works there himself to find out who was behind it.'

Alex swung round, frowning. 'What do you mean there's been a leak now? I thought the engine was due to be unveiled weeks ago. That was the reason Jordan Lang gave for holding me in that house—so he could keep me out of circulation—and he only set a time limit of one week on that, not several!'

Kenny shook his head. 'They had to change their plans at the last moment. Seems there was a design fault—nothing major, but enough to cause concern. One or two of the larger investors weren't too happy about it, but Mr Lang managed to talk them round and reassure them. However, one of our major competitors announced yesterday that they are about to launch an engine which has so many of the features of our prototype that there's no chance it can be coincidence. There's definitely been a leak of information and, as you can imagine, Jordan Lang is out for blood!'

And whose blood was it going to be? Alex didn't need to look very far to find the answer to that! He must have put two and two together very quickly, and come up with her as the major culprit. But there had to be something they could do—not just sit here waiting until he came gunning for them. After all, if Lang was interviewing people, then it proved he still had no idea as yet who she was. With a bit of nerve and a lot of luck, then maybe she and Kenny could weather this new storm safely.

She went and sat down facing Kenny, fixing a confident expression to her face. If they were going to outwit Jordan Lang, they would have to be confident and not panic.

'I take it you haven't been interviewed yet?'

'No. Fortunately I was sent out on a job today, and missed the first round; but I won't escape tomorrow, unless I ring in sick and wait until it all blows over.'

Alex shook her head, her eyes dark with certainty. 'This won't blow over. No, you have to go in tomorrow or you'll make people suspicious.'

'But you have no idea what Lang can be like! I can't do it, Lexie. He'll make mincemeat out of me!'

'I have a very good idea what he's like! Don't forget I had the pleasure of his company for several hours.'

Kenny had the grace to look discomfited. 'Yes, I know. I'm sorry. But can't you see how hopeless it all is? He'll never believe we were putting those blueprints back. He'll pin this whole leak on us, and it'll be prison ... if he doesn't take his own revenge first!'

There was a mounting hysteria in Kenny's voice, and Alex knew she had to stop it now. Everything was down to him now, and she wouldn't let him fall apart and ruin both their lives.

'He won't pin anything on us if you keep your head, Kenny. Jordan Lang doesn't know we are related, and there is no way he will unless you tell him. It's all down to you now, brother. Don't let me down.'

He looked up, forcing a smile. 'I'll try, Lexie. Believe me, I shall try!'

'But that isn't what I ordered! I ordered a brooch made out of those lovely Mexican fire opals you showed me.'

The indignation in the customer's voice cut short Alex's musings. Murmuring an apology, she hurried back to the workroom, and opened one of the shallow metal drawers where she stored her completed orders, and checked the details. It had been her mistake, mixing one client's surname with another's. It was the third mistake she'd made that morning, and it wasn't even lunchtime. She would have to get her head together and stop worrying about what was happening at the factory. Kenny would be all right—he'd had enough practice getting himself out of sticky situations, after all!.

While the customer wrote out a cheque, Alex slid the brooch into one of the elegant black leather boxes she used solely for her handcrafted jewellery, smoothing a finger lovingly over the gold-embossed legend, 'Alexandra', on its lid. It had taken years of hard work and effort to get to this point, but every time she sold something and packed it into one of these special boxes it made it all worthwhile.

There was a lull after the customer left, and Alex locked the display cases, and hurried through to the back to get on with some of the other orders. There was a bead curtain separating the workroom from the shop so she could easily hear if anyone came in. She set to work on yet another of the topaz scarf-clips which were still in such demand, calling out that she would only be a moment, when the shop bell tinkled, announcing the arrival of another customer. The sound of the beads rattling together as the curtain was pushed aside startled her, and she swung round, the cold rebuke at the interruption freezing unspoken on her lips.

'Surprised to see me, Jane? I don't know why. I did tell you I would find you, didn't I?'

'I...I...' She licked her dry lips, forcing her reeling senses to cope with his sudden appearance, then shook her head, wondering if she was hallucinating. But no hallucination had ever looked as dreadfully real as Jordan Lang did!

'What are you doing here?'

'What, Jane, no "how nice to see you again, Jordan", or "how have you been?" Tut-tut, not a very gracious way to greet an old friend who's gone to so much trouble to find you!'

'You're no *friend* of mine, Jordan Lang!' she snapped, stung into replying by the mockery in his voice. She stood up abruptly, holding tightly to the work-bench as her knees threatened to buckle. 'What do you want?'

'I would have thought that was obvious, especially to an intelligent businesswoman like you, Jane—or should I call you Alexandra?' He rolled the name round his tongue, as though savouring the sound of it, then smiled, and Alex felt her heart beat a little faster when she saw the expression in his eyes. 'Mmm, yes, I rather like it. I can't imagine why you were so reluctant to tell me what it was before. But then, I must confess that you will always hold a rather special place in my feelings as Jane Doe. Few women have ever left such a lasting impression on me as you did!'

He stepped further into the room, his eyes sweeping over the tools of her trade laid out on the bench before coming back to rest on her, and, despite herself, Alex shrank back from the anger in his gaze. 'Why? Tell me, why did you risk all this?

Was it just for money, or what? Damn you, woman, tell me! It's the least you owe me after all the trouble you've caused!' He moved suddenly, catching hold of her by the shoulders before she had a chance to evade his grasp. 'Why?'

'Let me go! You can't come in here and man-handle me, Jordan Lang!'

'And who's going to stop me? Your precious brother? Sorry to disappoint you, lady, but he won't be coming to your aid yet awhile. I've made certain of that!'

'What do you mean? What have you done to him?' There was a shrill note of concern in her voice. She twisted and turned, fighting to break away from the merciless grip; but he was too strong for her, as she knew already to her cost.

'Nothing...yet. And I shan't do anything if you and I can come to a satisfactory agreement.'

'What sort of an agreement? Damn you, Jordan, let me go!'

He smiled, scant amusement in his expression, just an icy coldness which made answering shivers trickle down her spine. 'I'm glad to hear you've decided to drop the formal title. Jordan sounds much more appropriate in view of the circumstances.'

'What circumstances? Stop trying to frighten me. Look, I know how bad it all looks, but Kenny and I had nothing at all to do with the leak of information.'

'And do you really expect me to believe that? Do you?' He shook her, not hard, not roughly, but with a restrained violence which was far more scary, hinting at the seething anger she could sense beneath the tight rein he had on his emotions. 'Your treachery has almost cost me the lot—the factory, the business, the whole damned lot! But you're going to make amends for what you've done. I'll make sure of that!'

'How?' Alex glared up at him, fear adding a depth to her own anger. He was so pig-headed, so set on believing the worst and staying blind to the truth. Fury at his unreasonable attitude made her goad him. 'And what exactly are you planning to do, Jordan? How shall you make me pay?'

She laid a nasty emphasis on his name, ignoring the way his grey eyes darkened ominously when he heard it. If he wanted her to use his given name, then she would do so, but it wouldn't stop the dozen or so more fitting ones from flying round inside her head. 'Come along now; don't be shy. What is it to be—prison? Financial ruin? I'm sure you've spent hours thinking up a fitting revenge for this crime I'm supposed to have committed.'

'Marriage.'

The word echoed round the room, softly, gently, yet with the impact of a speeding bullet. Alex stopped dead, her mouth dropping open just the barest fraction as she wondered if she'd misheard or, at least, misunderstood.

He laughed softly, the sound rippling round, filling her head with noise, her body with a feeling of unrelenting fear. 'Marriage,' he repeated quietly. He let go of her shoulders, his fingers warm and firm, sending a ripple of sensation coursing through her as he lifted her chin and snapped her mouth shut. 'You, Alexandra Campbell, are going to marry me.'

*　　*　　*

The coffee was hot, scalding her tongue and bringing tears to her eyes, but Alex welcomed the pain. All through the long minutes it had taken to lock the shop and lead Jordan upstairs to the flat, she'd had the feeling that she was in the middle of some horrible dream. Now the stinging pain of the coffee on her tongue brought her awake.

Her eyes lifted to the man sitting opposite, a steaming mug of coffee held in one large, well-shaped hand. While he was sitting like that, one leg crossed over the other, relaxed and doing something as mundane as drinking coffee, it was easy to be deceived into thinking he was much the same as other men: sane, rational, not given to crazy flights of fancy; but he wasn't. He had to be mad, stark raving mad, if he thought she was going to marry him!

She snorted in disgust, then felt the colour surge to her face when he looked up and met her eyes. Just for a second she held his gaze, feeling her pulse racing, then looked away, swirling the coffee from side to side in the cup. Her emotions felt like that, swinging back and forth, unable to find a level. One part of her wanted to dive right in and demand to know what he'd meant by the ridiculous statement, while the other side shied away from it with horror. Perhaps the safest way would be to lead up to finding the answer slowly.

'So, how did you find me? Did Kenny tell you?'

He shook his head, taking a long drink of the coffee before putting the cup down. 'No. I haven't seen your brother yet. I had him sent over to Yorkshire, to our other workshop, on some trumped-up excuse to get him out of the way. I didn't want him coming in here and breaking up our first meeting.'

Alex tried hard to ignore the mockingly intimate note in his deep voice, but for some silly reason her heart skipped a beat and let her down. 'Let's cut out the comedy, shall we, and just have the facts? If he didn't tell you, then how did you find me?'

'Sheer fluke, you might call it, though I prefer to see it as divine justice. I was at a friend's house last night, and she happened to be reading a magazine which featured an article about your jewellery. She made rather a point of showing it to me, in fact, possibly as a rather heavy-handed hint of what she'd like. I could hardly believe my eyes when I realised it was you. I've spent weeks trying to trace you, and there it is—a photograph plus a write-up on the Alexandra Campbell success story.' His mouth tightened, and he leaned forwards, all pretence at being relaxed forgotten.

'Is that what you planned to do with the money you got from selling the information—invest it in your business? Or was it to keep up with your brother's gambling habits?' He laughed softly when she started in surprise. 'Oh, yes, I know all about that. I've spent the night and the whole of the morning looking into your affairs, and there is nothing I don't know about the pair of you!'

'Then you must know that Kenny has stopped gambling and that he doesn't owe a penny to anyone!'

'I do know. But I also know what it cost you to pay off those debts, that the bank has been thinking seriously of foreclosing on the loan you have for this shop. The money you've been paid must have gone a long way to help you out of that!'

'No! You have it all wrong! All right, so Kenny did take the blueprints that day; but it was just a silly impulse. Once he came to his senses and realised what he'd done, he decided to put them back. That was what I was doing that night— putting them back...not stealing them!' He had to believe her, he just had to! But, looking at his grim face, Alex knew he didn't. She stood up, some vague idea of running from the room and away from the accusation in his eyes filling her head, but Jordan was at the door before she could take a step across the room.

'Sit down!'

She hesitated, a vein of caution responding to the harsh authority in his voice, yet warring with a desire to tell him to go to hell.

'I said sit down! I'm through wasting time like this. If you have any sense, then I suggest you sit back down and listen to what I have to say.'

Alex sank back on to the chair, gripping the arms with whitened knuckles. In silence she watched as Jordan sat down again, his eyes sweeping assessingly over the slender, elegant lines of her body, before coming to rest on the gleaming golden softness of her hair with an expression she found hard to define yet which made her feel strangely breathless.

'You are a very attractive woman, Alexandra, and you should be glad of it, because it means there just might be a solution to all this havoc you've caused.'

Alex said nothing, mainly because there was nothing she could say. She stared back at him, her eyes inky-dark against the ashen pallor of her face. Just for the moment he seemed to hesitate, as though something about her expression bothered him, but it was only a momentary lapse before he continued in that same calm, ruthless tone which flicked at her raw nerves like a whip.

'Thanks to what you and your brother have done, three of our major investors have withdrawn from the project. Without their backing the viability of the whole business is at stake. I took a gamble, you see, and sank everything into this project, and if it fails that will be it... the end of Lang's.'

She could understand why he was angry; given similar circumstances she would feel the same. But she still couldn't understand where she fitted in.

'I'm sorry,' she said quietly. 'I know you don't believe that I had nothing to do with the leak, but apart from that I can't see how marr... marr...' Her tongue tripped over the word, unable to breathe life and substance into such a crazy idea. However, it seemed that he had none of her reservations.

'Marriage, Alexandra. Don't be shy about saying it. The sooner you get used to the idea, the better it will be for everyone concerned—you, me, and your precious brother!'

There was such harshness in his voice that she shuddered, looking away from the mesmeric gaze of his silvery eyes as she tried to think what to do or what to say, but it was impossible while that word kept filling her mind. Marriage. To Jordan Lang. Just the thought made her heart beat wildly in a heavy throbbing rhythm, sending the blood coursing through her veins. She knew she should laugh in his face and tell him in no uncertain terms that there was no way she would marry him, but something in the depths of his eyes frightened her into silence.

'No objections? I had imagined that you would be opposed to the idea at first, but it seems I was wrong. Maybe the idea of us being joined in marriage isn't completely unappealing to you?'

He was goading her, quite deliberately and, while Alex knew it, she couldn't prevent the heated retort from rising to her lips to chase away the numbness.

'I have no objections. There is no need for any objections because the whole idea is ridiculous! There is no way I will ever marry you, Jordan Lang, not if you were the last man on earth!'

'Really? Mmm, it could be interesting trying to overcome those feelings, but unfortunately I don't have time to take you up on such a challenge. You owe me a lot for all the damage you've done, Alexandra Campbell, and I intend to see that you pay every last penny of the debt!'

'And how does marriage come into it?' She leaned forwards to glare at him across the space of a couple of inches. 'Surely resorting to threats to find yourself a wife is going a bit far, though I can understand that any woman with an ounce of sense would be reluctant to get involved with a man like you ... Ohh!'

She cried out in alarm as he caught her hands and pulled her to him so abruptly that she fell to her knees at his feet.

'So you don't think any woman would want me?' His voice was low and filled with a note which should have warned her to reply with caution, but Alex had gone way beyond the point of caution.

'No! No woman in her right mind would want you!'

A light flared into his eyes, hot, bright, burning with an intensity she could almost feel as he swept his gaze over the flushed contours of her face. Suddenly terrified at what he was going to do, she started to struggle, but she was no match for his far superior strength, and could only watch helplessly as he held her and bent forwards until his mouth touched hers. She moaned, an anguished little cry which faded abruptly into nothing as she felt the delicate touch of his lips barely brushing hers, then the warm moistness of his tongue tracing the outline of her lips in a whisper-soft caress which made every cell in her body tingle. Expecting a brutal assault, a punishment for her temerity, she stilled, her body clenching in shock and sensation as his tongue circled her lips time after time, tracing over the soft curves, lingering to probe at the join of her lips, then moving on before she could either refuse or allow entry.

Slowly Jordan drew back, his face unreadable as he studied the red moistness of her mouth, the faint trembling she couldn't quite hide. She'd been kissed before, many times, and far more passionately, but not once had her senses been stirred as this tantalising brushing of his mouth on hers had done.

'Do you still think you're right? That no woman would ever want me?' His voice was deep, soft, stroking over her sensitised nerves like warm velvet, and she shuddered, summoning up every last scrap of control she had.

'Yes. I'm right!'

'Are you sure, Alex? One hundred per cent certain?' He raised his hand and ran a gentle finger across her mouth, tracing the outline just as his tongue had done. Alex held herself rigid, fighting to control the shudders which threatened to destroy her control at the evocative touch. Once, twice, three times he retraced the same disturbing path, then gently parted her lips to run a fingertip slowly over the soft inner flesh of her lower lip. 'I think you need convincing, that's all.'

'No! Jordan, no, I don't want...'

With a swiftness she hadn't expected he bent his head and took her mouth again, sliding his tongue between her parted lips to tangle with hers in a heady, sensual rhythm which made the blood surge in her veins. Suddenly, shockingly, she was on fire, burning up, consumed by the mastery of the kiss, the intensity of feeling he was igniting inside her. That first slow caress had been the spark, and now her emotions were alight and burning out of control.

Caught up in the kiss, Alex was unaware of the exact moment when he loosened his grip on her arms, yet achingly aware of the feel of his fingers sliding under her hair to stroke the soft skin at the nape of her neck. She could so easily have pulled away and put an end to the kiss, but there was no thought of that in her head, just as there was no thought of resisting when he pulled her into the cradle made by his wide-spread legs and pressed her closer against the hardness of his body. Her eyelids fluttered shut, and she reached up to run her hands over the cool, silky hair at the back of his head while she kissed him back.

The abruptness of the rejection as he pushed her from him stunned her, so that for a moment she couldn't understand what was happening.

'Open your eyes!'

His voice was cold and harsh, cutting through the lingering heat of passion. Slowly, Alex opened her eyes, feeling the colour drain from her face as she saw the expression in his eyes.

'Are you still so sure that no woman would want me?'

There was relentless cruelty in the question, and Alex gasped, turning her head away, feeling sick. How could she have been such a fool as to fall for that and let him trick her in that despicable way? That kiss, which had promised a glimpse of heaven, had been founded in hell; it had been nothing to him apart from a means of teaching her a lesson.

Cold waves of embarrassment flooded through her, and she started to scramble to her feet; but she should have realised that Jordan would never let her off the hook until he had embedded it as deeply as possible in her flesh. Catching hold of her chin between his thumb and forefinger, he forced her to meet his eyes.

'Be honest, Alexandra; didn't *you* want me just now?'

There was something in his voice, something besides the harshness, and just for a moment Alex felt her body tremble with a lingering echo of passion before she came abruptly to her senses. She dragged her chin away and stood up, her face cold with contempt and a trace of pain she couldn't quite hide.

'This has gone far enough. I have neither the time nor the inclination to play any more silly games with you, Jordan. I suggest that you either tell me what you want or leave!'

'I'm not playing games. This whole thing has gone way past the point of being a game. However, I must agree that we have wasted enough time. I've already outlined the predicament the company is in, thanks to you; however, there is a chance that I can save it with more investment. And that is where you come in.'

He stood up and walked to the window, pushing the curtains aside to look out, and if Alex hadn't known better she would have said that he was weighing up his next words before continuing; but why? In his own mind, Jordan had already tried and convicted her; all that was left now was for him to pronounce sentence, and she couldn't see *that* causing him a problem! Tension hummed through her as she waited to hear what he would say, and she clenched her hands into fists, fighting to keep a grip on her control.

He swung round suddenly, the light from the window bouncing blue sparks off his night-dark hair, yet setting his face into shadow, so that Alex couldn't see his expression. But she had no need to. She knew what he thought of her. He'd made it quite plain both with words and with that devastatingly cruel kiss, yet she couldn't prevent the sudden pain which knifed through her heart at the thought of just how much he must dislike her.

Anger that she should feel that way ran through her, stiffening her spine, adding a strength to her voice. 'You know that I have no money, so what exactly are you suggesting? That I should steal someone else's secrets and sell them to pay you back?'

Jordan stiffened at her tone, taking a half-step forwards before seeming to force himself to relax. 'Smart answers aren't going to get us anywhere. I have all the money I need to see this project through to completion and put the company back on target. It is just a question of gaining access to it.'

'Then you intend to go ahead and market the engine?' There was relief in Alex's voice as she asked the question.

'Yes. Why? Are you disappointed that you have failed? You were just a shade premature, you see. We didn't discover the flaws in the design until *after* your visit to the factory, which means that our competitors don't have the benefit of knowing what further modifications we have made. It should take them some time to sort it all out, so for now we are still in the lead, and can carry on as planned.'

'Then I still don't see where I fit in. Why do you need me?'

'It's simple. When my mother died a few months ago she left me her personal fortune in trust to be handed over either when I reached the age of thirty-five, or in the event of my marrying. I shall be thirty-five in six months' time, but I can't wait that long. It's vital that I have the money now!'

'But why marry me to get it? There must be other women who would be pleased to marry you— women you know!'

'Because we both know exactly where we stand and what the marriage is for. I have neither the time nor the inclination to go through all the ritual another woman would expect before she agreed to the marriage, neither do I want a wife who would expect me to dance attendance on her. The only thing I'm interested in right now is getting the firm out of trouble!'

'And when that's done you won't need the en-cumbrance of a wife?' Alex asked shrewdly.

'Precisely. A divorce will be easy enough to obtain. However, I want this marriage to appear as genuine as possible while it lasts. I don't want any more of our investors pulling their money out be-cause they've found out that Lang's back is up against the wall.'

'And how long do you envisage this "marriage" lasting?'

He shrugged. 'Six months at most. After that we could let it be known that we had decided to sep-arate, and that's it. Divorce is common enough nowadays to cause little comment.'

He had it all worked out, all the steps written down from one to ten. Alex didn't know what dis-gusted her most—the thought of what he was pre-pared to do to get what he wanted, or the ice-coldness of his mind for coming up with such a plan. But one thing he hadn't allowed for was that she wasn't going to be a neatly numbered step in anyone's plan!

She swung round and marched to the door and opened it. 'Get out. You were crazy for coming here and expecting me to agree with such a ridiculous proposal.'

'Was I? I don't think so. I'd say you are the crazy one if you refuse and accept the alternative.'

'What alternative? Are you threatening me?'

'If you prefer to hear it stated bluntly, then yes, I am.' In a few long strides he crossed the room and closed the door, leaning against it as he studied her face. Alex tried her hardest to meet his eyes with an outward show of composure, but it was no more than a few seconds before she was forced to look away, terrified by the determination she could see in his expression.

'And if I do refuse, then what do you intend to do?'

'What any law-abiding citizen would do, of course—go to the police and have you and your brother charged with industrial espionage. I'm not absolutely certain what sentence the charge carries, but I imagine you would both be facing roughly two to five years in prison.'

'Two to five years? You can't prove anything,' she cried desperately, 'you know you can't! It will be your word against ours.'

'That's where you're wrong. I already have the sworn statement of one of the security guards that your brother was in the factory that night. He was only too eager to tell me everything he knew once I'd...pointed out to him the gravity of the situation.'

Poor Sid. He must have been terrified when Jordan had questioned him. It was little wonder he had admitted letting Kenny into the factory. But that still wasn't proof—not enough to convince a jury, surely?

'And, of course, there is the other charge to be taken into consideration.'

Alex shot him a swift glance, but it was impossible to second-guess him. 'What other charge?'

'Assault.' He ran a hand over his head, his eyes pinning hers with a steely intensity. 'Surely you haven't forgotten that bump on the head you gave me? I have medical records to prove that I suffered a mild concussion from that.'

'But I didn't hit you!' she exclaimed, horrified that he should be trying to blame the accident on her.

'That's debatable, but it makes no difference when I have a witness who will testify that you went and asked him to fetch a doctor for me after spending time up at the house, *and* that when they got there they found me semi-conscious on the settee. You remember Owen, don't you, Alexandra? I'm sure he remembers you, and can testify to your identity.'

Of course she remembered Owen. She'd stopped at his house and roused him from his bed to get him to call a doctor for Jordan that night. Now she wished she'd never bothered. She should have driven off in the jeep and let Jordan Lang rot!

'I can ruin you, Alexandra Campbell, both you and your brother. Oh, maybe there is a slim chance that you will be able to talk yourself out of any charges I bring, but can you handle the publicity, and the fact that I will make it my business to see that you suffer—that neither you nor Kenny will be able to earn a living or hold your heads up again?'

'You can't do that! You haven't that much in-
fluence.' It was more a plea for reassurance than a
refutal of what he'd said, and Alex felt a shudder
inch its way along her backbone as she saw the way
Jordan smiled, saw the expression in the depths of
his eyes.

'Haven't I? I wouldn't bank on that. Shall I get
on the telephone now and call a few of your suppliers, and tell them that you are no longer a good
risk? Or shall I call the bank and suggest that they
should think about calling in their loan, as there is
a strong possibility that you will be facing police
charges soon? It wouldn't take much. Just a quiet
word in the right ears and then your business will
be no more than a memory.'

'You'd do that?' Her voice was a mere whisper,
but he heard it. He lifted her chin with a decep-
tively gentle finger, and looked straight into her
horrified eyes.

'Yes, I'd do it. That and more if I had to.
Whatever it takes to get what I want. So tell me
what it's to be. Prison and financial ruin, or
marriage?'

'I . . . I can't tell you now! I need time to think,'
she cried desperately.

'There is no time, that's the whole point. Thanks
to what you have done, I need to start immediately
if I intend to save the business. So what is it to be—
yes or no?'

His fingers tightened on her chin, bruising the
soft flesh, but Alex was scarcely aware of the discomfort. She closed her eyes, trying desperately to
find another way out of the mess, but all she could
see were the vivid pictures Jordan had painted of

her future. Could she really condemn both her and Kenny to prison followed by a life of poverty? Yet she couldn't bring herself to agree.

'There must be another way, Jordan. Please!' Her eyes opened and stared straight into his, holding desperation, but there was no softening in the steely gaze, no hint of forgiveness or understanding.

'There is no other way. None! So make your choice.'

'And if I do agree, then do you promise you'll drop the charges, that you won't ruin my business, and that Kenny won't be sacked?'

He shrugged. 'Yes, of course I do. Your business will be safe, and as for your brother—well, I can hardly sack my wife's brother, can I? It would look very odd.'

'Then . . . yes!'

The word slid from her lips almost before she realised she was saying it, and she caught her breath, wishing she could call it back. Just for a moment Jordan was silent, a strange expression on his face as he studied her; then he nodded.

'Good. I'm glad you decided to see sense in the end.' He released her chin, his knuckles brushing softly across her mouth, his voice very deep and liquid. 'You never know, Alexandra, this could turn out to be quite a pleasant experience for us after all.'

Alex's face flamed as she caught his meaning, and remembered how she'd responded with such abandon to that kiss. For a tiny second sensation curled through her, heating her veins, sending the blood swirling through her in a fierce tide of longing before she forced the memories from her mind.

'Go to hell, Jordan Lang!' she said, her voice almost breaking.

He laughed, swinging the door open as he prepared to leave. 'I said it once before, and I may as well repeat it: wherever I go you go too. I guess it applies even more now than ever before. Man and wife, Alexandra. Think about it!'

He left, leaving the door open behind him. For a moment Alex stayed quite still, staring at the empty doorway, feeling her pulse racing wildly. Man and wife. Oh, she would think about it all right, would think about little else, in fact. Just the idea should have shocked her rigid, sent her running screaming into hiding. So why did she feel this crazy little spark of excitement deep inside?

CHAPTER FIVE

A CAR horn sounded in the street below, and Alex jumped, dropping the earring she'd been holding. It fell to the floor and lay in a glittering little heap on the carpet, but she made no move to pick it up. Crossing the room, she parted the curtains and looked down into the street, her heart leaping in a sickening surge as she recognised the trimly elegant lines of Jordan's car parked outside.

She dropped the curtain abruptly into place, and turned away to stare round the room with hunted eyes, but there was nothing there to offer help or comfort, nothing that could put an end to this nightmare. Even Kenny was away from home, sent to the Yorkshire factory on Jordan's specific instructions. He hadn't wanted to go, and it had taken all Alex's powers of persuasion to make him. Now she wished she hadn't. She could have done with him being here to bolster her flagging courage.

The horn sounded again, longer, louder, with a barely concealed impatience in its strident tone, and with a cold feeling of inevitability she picked up her coat and bag and left the flat, running down the stairs to let herself out through the shop.

Jordan had already got out of the car, and was walking towards the door when she appeared. He stopped and waited for her to join him on the pavement, his face devoid of any expression.

'I was beginning to think you weren't coming,' he said shortly, his eyes sweeping over her pale face.

'I wish I wasn't.' She swept past him and stood next to the car, staring along the quiet street, focusing all her attention on the darkness barely broken by the dim glow of the streetlights. A light wind was blowing, rustling the few leaves left on the trees as it shook the branches, making flickering patterns dance across the pools of light, and Alex shivered as it curled coldly round her face and neck.

'Come along. Get in, or we'll be late.'

Jordan opened the car door and held it for her while she slid inside, before striding round to the driver's side. He started the engine and set the car into gear, flicking a quick glance sideways at her before he pulled away from the kerb.

'I hope you don't intend to make any waves tonight. This evening has been arranged specifically to announce our engagement, and I won't tolerate you trying to pull any of your tricks.'

His tone was cold, the words clipped, but they left surprisingly little impression on Alex. The coldness seemed to be spreading, numbing her senses, making it impossible to feel anything but a faint surprise that this was really happening. She felt detached, alienated from everything, as though she were standing outside herself watching what was going on.

'Did you hear me?'

Rough impatience tinged Jordan's voice now as he slid the car round a tight bend then picked up speed as they left the town behind. Alex glanced sideways at him, her eyes running impersonally over his clean-cut profile, the smooth sweep of his dark hair; but she felt nothing—not anger, not attraction...nothing.

'Yes, I heard you,' she said quietly, her voice flat. 'You don't need to worry. I know what is expected of me.'

He swore softly, his hands tightening round the steering-wheel, his lips compressing. 'Then is it too much to ask that you try to show a bit more enthusiasm? This is supposed to be a wonderful occasion for both of us, but one look at you and no one is going to believe that!'

'Is that really so surprising? This wasn't my idea, remember? This was your little plan, from start to finish, so you'll have to forgive me if I appear less than "enthusiastic"!' There was a faint bite to her voice now as she felt the first stirrings of anger nibbling away at the edges of the coldness.

'It might have been my idea, but it was only necessary because of your meddling. I don't like the idea any more than you do, but I have no choice.'

'Of course you have a choice. Why are you being so blind? Why can't you open your eyes and look at the facts and see the truth?'

'Meaning?'

'Meaning that I didn't steal your information and neither did Kenny. You're just using us as scapegoats while the real culprit goes free. You would be better employed trying to find who really is responsible than in forcing me to go through with this ridiculous charade.'

He laughed bitterly. 'So we're back to that, are we? Still protesting your innocence and claiming that you are the wronged party? Forgive me, but I'm afraid I don't believe it any more now than I did a few weeks ago at the house!'

'You don't want to believe it! You don't want to look for the truth in case you have to admit you're wrong! That's what this is all about really. The fact that the great Jordan Lang can never be wrong!'

There was angry scorn in her voice as she spat the accusation at him, but he appeared unmoved as he slid her a level glance.

'I can be wrong the same as anyone can, but I'm not wrong about this. You can say what you like, but I will never believe that you are anything but guilty!'

He turned back to concentrate on driving the powerful car along the narrow road, and Alex rested her head back against the seat and closed her eyes in defeat. It had been a waste of time trying to convince him that he'd made a mistake. If anything, it had only hardened his opinion of her and served to destroy that merciful numbness which might have helped her through the evening. Now she was back to square one, back to feeling these cold little tremors of fear in the pit of her stomach, which she'd been living with ever since Jordan had come to the shop and told her his plan. There had to be a way to convince him that he couldn't force her into this unwanted marriage, but so far she'd not managed to find out how.

In total silence they drove on through the night until Jordan slowed the car and swung in through a pair of ornate wrought-iron gates and along a winding driveway. Alex opened her eyes and looked round, feeling her heart bumping painfully in her

NO RISK, NO OBLIGATION TO BUY ... NOW OR EVER!

CASINO JUBILEE
"Scratch'n Match" Game

Here's how to play:

1. Peel off label from front cover. Place it in space provided at right. With a coin, carefully scratch off the silver box. This makes you eligible to receive two or more free books, and possibly another gift, depending upon what is revealed beneath the scratch-off area.

2. You'll receive brand-new Harlequin Romance® novels. When you return this card, we'll rush you the books and gift you qualify for, ABSOLUTELY FREE!

3. Then, if we don't hear from you, every month we'll send you 6 additional novels to read and enjoy, months before they are available in bookstores. You can return them and owe nothing, but if you decide to keep them, you'll pay only $2.24* each plus 25¢ delivery and applicable sales tax, if any*. That's the complete price, and— compared to cover prices of $2.89 each in stores—quite a bargain!

4. When you join the Harlequin Reader Service®, you'll get our subscribers-only newsletter, as well as additional free gifts from time to time, just for being a subscriber!

5. You must be completely satisfied. You may cancel at any time simply by sending us a note or a shipping statement marked ''cancel'' or by returning any shipment to us at our cost.

YOURS FREE!

This lovely heart-shaped box is richly detailed with cut-glass decorations, perfect for holding a precious memento or keepsake—and it's yours absolutely free when you accept our no-risk offer.

CASINO JUBILEE
"Scratch'n Match" Game

SCRATCH HERE

PLACE LABEL HERE

?

CHECK CLAIM CHART BELOW
FOR YOUR FREE GIFTS!

YES! I have placed my label from the front cover in the space provided above and scratched off the silver box. Please send me all the gifts for which I qualify. I understand I am under no obligation to purchase any books, as explained on the opposite page.

116 CIH AG5E (U-H-R-02/93)

Name _____

Address _____ Apt. _____

City _____ State _____ Zip _____

CASINO JUBILEE CLAIM CHART		
🍒🍒🍒	WORTH 4 FREE BOOKS AND A FREE HEART-SHAPED CURIO BOX	
🍒🔔🍒	WORTH 3 FREE BOOKS	
🍒🔔🍒	WORTH 2 FREE BOOKS	CLAIM N° 1528

◄ DETACH AND MAIL CARD TODAY! ►

▼ DETACH AND MAIL CARD TODAY! ▼

BUSINESS REPLY MAIL
FIRST CLASS MAIL   PERMIT NO. 717   BUFFALO, NY

POSTAGE WILL BE PAID BY ADDRESSEE

HARLEQUIN READER SERVICE
3010 WALDEN AVE
PO BOX 1867
BUFFALO NY 14240-9952

NO POSTAGE
NECESSARY
IF MAILED
IN THE
UNITED STATES

chest as she watched the lights of the restaurant coming closer and closer.

'Have you been here before?' He slid the car into a parking space and cut the engine, turning slightly to look at her so that the lights spilling from the huge arched windows made a silvery backdrop for his darkly handsome features. Alex shook her head, glancing round the crowded car park at the expensive collection of cars, feeling sick. Now that the moment was here, when she must go into that building and be introduced as Jordan's fiancée, she felt terrified, waves of fear curling and rolling in her stomach, making her dizzy with the sheer force of them. It took every ounce of strength she possessed to stop herself leaping from the car and running screaming into the night.

'I think you should enjoy it. The Country Club is renowned for serving some of the best food in the northwest. I can vouch for that. But before we go inside there are one or two things we need to get straight.'

'What sort of things?' Alex's voice was a rough husky rasp of sound, and she felt him look at her, but she refused to meet his gaze in case it snapped that last thread of control she was clinging desperately to.

'Just a few basics which people are bound to ask about. I've made a note of everything you'll need to know. Date and time of the wedding, et cetera. It's all booked for three weeks' time. I had hoped to get it over with sooner, but unfortunately the banns had to be called, so that was the earliest that could be managed without making it look too rushed.' He slid a hand into the pocket of his suit jacket, pulled out a folded slip of paper, and held it out to her. Alex stared at it, her eyes dark with a growing horror. He'd told her that the wedding had to take place as soon as possible, but never in her wildest imaginings had she expected this sort of time limit!

She looked up, the refusal hovering unspoken on her lips as she met his eyes and read the ruthless determination in their depths.

'Don't even think about it. You made your decision the other day, and there's no way I am letting you back out!'

'But can't you see how crazy it all is? It's the sort of thing you read about in books, but people don't get married for this kind of reason!'

There was a desperate plea for understanding, but it was obvious that he was unmoved by it. He smiled coldly, dropping the piece of paper on to her lap.

'People get married for any number of reasons. I would have thought you were old enough to appreciate that.'

'Maybe they do, but I don't have to be one of them.' She drew in a ragged breath, willing herself to stay calm and not let it deteriorate into a verbal battle. 'Look, Jordan, I can appreciate why you are so angry, but this isn't the way to solve your problems. It isn't!'

'As far as I am concerned it is, and that's that! End of the discussion.' He turned away to open the car door, but Alex couldn't let him get away with it that easily. She caught his arm, forcing him to turn back and look at her.

'And what happens if I refuse to go through with the wedding? What do you propose to do then, take a shot-gun and force me up the aisle?' She laughed wildly, verging on hysteria. 'What a turn-up for the book that would be. Jordan Lang forcing a woman into marrying him!'

Jordan's face darkened, the muscles under her fingers going rigid, and Alex felt the laughter die in her throat almost as quickly as it had begun.

'I don't need anything as crude as a gun. Have you forgotten so quickly that I hold all the cards, and can play them as I choose? But if it makes you feel better about this marriage, then maybe this will help.' He pulled her to him, holding her tightly as he tipped her head back, his fingers twined in the long strands of her hair.

'Let me go!' she ordered, but he just laughed, his eyes burning with an intensity which made a hot little quiver race through her body, draining the strength from her limbs.

'You know you don't really mean that. Don't you remember the other day, how it felt when I kissed you, held you, felt your heart beating under mine as it's doing now?' He slid his hand up to lie under her breasts so that Alex could feel the rapid beating of her heart pulsing against his palm. 'Remember how you enjoyed it? If you feel so badly about this marriage, then maybe you would prefer it to become more like a real one, based on mutual attraction rather than pure convenience?'

'No! You're mad if you think I'd ever——'

She got no further, as his head swooped down and he covered her parted lips, kissing her with a heat and passion which left her breathless and trembling within the space of seconds. But she couldn't let him do this, wouldn't let him subdue her by passion as he had before with threats. When he raised his head she forced her trembling, swollen lips to repeat the denial.

'No! No...'

He took her mouth again, his tongue sliding between her parted lips, tangling with hers so that the denial was lost, only echoing in her head until that too became lost in the magic he was creating. She couldn't seem to think, just feel, as though every one of her senses had been heightened to an unbearable degree. The silky touch of his tongue sliding against hers, the taste of his lips, the rapid beating of his heart—or was it hers?—the faint, warmly fragrant smell of his skin, the rainbows of colour flashing behind her closed lids...

He drew back slowly, studying her flushed face, and Alex had the feeling that he was searching for some kind of an answer to some unspoken question, before he smiled, that old familiar taunting smile, and the impression was gone.

'See what I mean? It would be no great hardship for either of us. I may not like your moral values, but I would be a liar if I said I wasn't attracted to you.'

How she hated him! She dragged herself out of his arms, her blue eyes burning. 'Forget it! There is no way this is ever going to be anything other than a business arrangement!'

He laughed shortly, raising a hand to run it over his dark hair, and smooth it back from his forehead. 'That's fine by me. In fact, I've had a pre-nuptial agreement drawn up by my solicitor, outlining what we can both expect from this marriage. I shall arrange for you to sign it as soon as possible. Now I think we had better go in and meet our guests. They'll be wondering where we are if... Oh, I forgot. You'd better have this first.'

He reached into his pocket again and pulled out a small leather-covered box, snapping on the interior car light before handing it to her. Alex stared at it in silence, feeling something cold and hard welling in the pit of her stomach, knowing that there was no way she could open the box and examine its contents.

'Aren't you going to open it? Let me do it, then.'

He took it back from her unresisting fingers, easing the lid open before presenting it to her again. 'An engagement wouldn't be real without a ring. I hope I've got the right size, but I'm sure it can be altered. You'd better try it on and see.'

He lifted the huge solitaire diamond off its black velvet cushion, catching hold of her cold hand to slide it up her finger in a travesty of an engagement being cemented. Alex stared down at it, watching the way the huge stone caught the dim light and bounced flashes of icy fire back. It was a magnificent stone, flawless, perfectly cut and set, and she hated it with an intensity which surprised her. Something of what she felt must have shown on her face because Jordan's eyes narrowed.

'I was told it was a perfect gem,' he said harshly. 'The jeweller assured me that I would have to go a long way to find its equal.'

Alex shrugged, feeling the solid weight of the ring like an alien presence on her finger, unasked for and definitely unwanted. 'He wasn't lying. It's rare to find such a perfect stone nowadays.'

'Then why do I have the distinct impression that you don't like it?'

'Do you? How strange. However, I must admit that I'm not thrilled about being responsible for such a valuable piece of jewellery. I think it would be better if you took it back. I'm sure your friends will understand if we tell them that we haven't got round to buying the ring yet.'

She started to slide the ring from her finger, but he reached over and stopped her, his fingers biting cruelly into hers.

'Damn you, woman! Who do you think you are, turning your nose up at that ring? You're nothing but a common thief, and don't ever forget that! Do what you like with the ring. Consider it a bonus if you like. Once this fiasco is all over, then maybe what you get from selling it will stop you stealing from anyone else!'

It shouldn't have hurt to hear him say those things, shouldn't have felt like a knife stabbing into her heart; but it did. Alex pulled her hand away, and opened the car door to climb out, feeling the hot wash of tears behind her lids. Uncaring if he was following, she led the way towards the restaurant entrance, wondering if she would ever grow used to hearing what Jordan thought of her. Deep down, she knew his cruelty shouldn't hurt so much but, if she was really honest with herself, she had to admit that it did. The realisation frightened her, making her face the unpalatable fact that she was far more vulnerable to him than she wanted to be.

*   *   *

'Tell us, Alex, just how did you and Jordan meet and fall in love so quickly? It's come like a bolt out of the blue to all his friends, I can tell you. We thought he would never find the woman who would mean more to him than his beloved business!'

A ripple of laughter ran round the table, and slowly Alex laid her spoon aside as she looked round at the expectant faces. Apart from Jordan and James Morgan, the head project designer whom she'd met once before, she knew none of the other guests chosen to share this occasion. They had all been polite and friendly since she'd been introduced to them as Jordan's fiancée, but she'd been aware from the outset that they were openly curious about her sudden appearance in his life. The question now was, how was she going to satisfy that curiosity?

Her gaze slid on to the man seated opposite her, and she felt a flicker of satisfaction when she saw the expression of unease on his face. Obviously, Jordan was experiencing some doubts of his own about how she would answer, and suddenly the urge to pay him back for how he had hurt her with his loathsome comments became too strong to ignore. She smiled sweetly at him, a coquettish tilt to her lips.

'Shall I tell them, darling?' she murmured seductively. 'Or would you prefer it to remain our little secret?'

His eyes narrowed, the hand holding the wine glass tightening convulsively round its fragile stem before he seemed to force himself to relax and smile back at her.

'Tell everyone, by all means, darling,' he replied just as softly, 'but maybe not *all* the details. Some things are just too private ever to share.'

Was she the only one to hear the underlying note of threat in his voice? Alex shot a quick look round the table, and realised that she was. She hesitated, wondering if she was asking for more trouble than she could handle by carrying on, then caught a glimpse of the smugly complacent expression on Jordan's face and knew it would be worth it just to wipe it off!

'Jordan kidnapped me.'

The effect was riveting, everything she could have hoped for, and Alex knew the sight of all the stunned faces staring at her would go a long way to make up for whatever form his retribution took.

'I'm sorry, but did you actually say that Jordan...well, that he...?' The brunette tailed off, obviously wondering if she'd suffered some sort of a brainstorm, so Alex hastened to put her mind at rest.

'Mmm, that's right. Kidnapped me,' she repeated clearly, smiling brilliantly at her attentive audience before letting her eyes drift to Jordan with a hint of a challenge in their depths. 'Isn't that right, my love?'

All heads turned towards him, and Alex rested her chin on the heel of her hand as she waited to hear how he would answer.

'Perhaps I wouldn't have put it quite like that, *sweetheart*!' There was a faint edge in his voice, but Alex ignored it, staring limpidly back at him, her eyes as huge and guileless as she could make them.

'Wouldn't you?' She gave a soft, seductive little laugh. 'But what else can you call carrying me off in the middle of the night when we'd hardly met? Come on, *darling*, don't be shy about admitting what you did in front of your friends.'

The brunette was all eyes now, obviously hanging on every word, and Alex knew as clearly as she knew her own name that the story would be all over town before very long.

'But why? I mean, why would Jordan kidnap you? It's not the sort of thing he would usually do.'

Well, it was her own fault, of course; she should have known the sort of questions she'd be inviting by telling half the story. The trouble was she'd been so intent on making Jordan sweat a little that she'd not stopped to think where it could lead to. Uncertain how to get herself out of such a sticky explanation, she glanced at him and saw that he was watching her with a mocking expression on his face. Obviously, he'd realised just how successfully she'd backed herself into a corner, and was now prepared to sit back and watch her trying to struggle out! The realisation unlocked her tongue, giving her the strength to frame an answer of sorts.

'It was all a silly mix-up, really. I'd gone to the factory one night, and Jordan found me in there. He seemed to misunderstand my reasons for being there, so decided to teach me a lesson by carrying me off to his cottage in Wales, and...well, I'm sure I can leave the rest to your imaginations!'

There was a ripple of understanding laughter round the table, and she relaxed, pleased that she'd got out of the dilemma so neatly and with so little trouble. However, it appeared that not everyone was satisfied by her vague explanation.

'This mix-up you mentioned; can we take it that you managed to clear it up?'

James Morgan spoke directly to her for the first time that evening apart from a perfunctory greeting when they'd been introduced, and Alex forced herself to keep her smile in place. What was it about the man that she disliked? He had never been anything other than coolly polite to her when they'd met previously, yet there had been something about him then which had made her skin prickle with a vague feeling of animosity. Now, seeing the intent scrutiny he was subjecting her to, Alex felt it again with a renewed force. She hesitated before answering, wondering exactly how much he knew about what had happened. He was the firm's top designer, so it was possible that Jordan could have confided in him. But if he had, then surely he would be more concerned about glossing over the incident than in making an issue of it?

Undecided how to handle the question, Alex remained silent, then felt a surge of relief when the brunette spoke up again.

'Of course they must have sorted everything out! They are engaged to be married, aren't they? And in only three weeks' time! Oh, it's all so romantic—love at first sight, I bet; was it, Jordan?'

She turned to Jordan, who had been following the exchange, and Alex couldn't stop herself from looking at him too. Just for a moment their eyes met and held, and she felt her pulse leap and her breath catch at the warm glow of intimacy which flowed between them, the feeling of a secret only they knew and shared. Time seemed to stand still, holding them cocooned in one single never-ending heartbeat, then Jordan turned away, a strange fleeting expression crossing his face as he answered the question.

'Let's just say that I was completely bowled over by Alexandra that first night, and that she has made a huge impact on my life ever since.'

Disappointment welled inside her, and she dropped her eyes to the table, picking up her wine glass to take a swallow of the pale liquid, calling herself every kind of a fool. What had she expected him to say—that he *had* fallen in love with her that first night? The whole idea was crazy, just as she was crazy to feel as though she'd just been dealt some kind of a hurtful blow! With a defiant little tilt of the glass, she drained the last of the wine, then nearly choked when Jordan spoke softly beside her.

'I'd take it easy with that, if I were you. It might loosen your tongue even more, and I think you've said quite enough for one night.'

She looked up, her eyes widening as she saw him standing next to her. She'd been so intent on her own thoughts that she hadn't been aware of him getting up and coming round the table to her. Now she flinched as he slid a hand across her shoulder, smiling at her for the benefit of several of the guests who were openly watching them.

'Dance with me, darling?' he asked smoothly, his voice a fraction louder so that it would carry round the table. 'After all, this should be a night to remember.'

It would be that all right, and, if she had her way, Alex would have given *him* a night he would remember for a long time to come! A host of spiky comments hovered on the tip of her tongue, but she got no chance to utter even one of them, as he bent and pressed a hard kiss to her lips. A murmur of appreciation ran round the table at the openly loving gesture, but Alex wasn't in any position to appreciate the easy way with which he'd subdued her attempt at defiance. She glared at him, her blue eyes meeting his from the distance of a mere inch or two as he held the kiss, but he did no more than smile faintly so that she could feel his lips curving upwards as they pressed against hers. He drew back slowly, reaching out to push a long strand of golden hair behind her shoulder, his fingers lingering against her neck in a light touch which sent a sudden streak of fire licking along her veins. When he held his hand out to her, she slid her fingers into his and let him lead her on to the small dance-floor, too shaken by that sudden flare of sensation to summon up the strength to refuse.

They danced in silence for several minutes, Jordan's hand resting lightly at the small of her back as he guided her round the floor to the gentle rhythm of a waltz. Alex could feel the light brush of his hand even through the fabric of her dress, could feel the heat of his palm, the strength of his lean fingers, as though every nerve-ending had become sensitised to an incredible degree. What was the matter with her? Why was she acting like some...some lovesick schoolgirl?

The thought shocked her so much that she stumbled, losing the rhythm. Jordan steadied her, pulling her closer to avoid another couple who were dancing close behind them. Just for a moment Alex let herself rest against the hard, lean strength of his body, feeling the play of muscles under her hand where it pressed against his shoulder, then drew abruptly away.

'Sorry. I seemed to get in a bit of a tangle then.'

'It doesn't matter.' He looked down into her face, studying the twin patches of colour painted along her cheekbones in stark contrast to the underlying pallor. 'Are you feeling all right? You look rather flushed.'

'Such touching concern, Jordan. It does you credit, but of course it's only right and proper that you should be concerned about your new fiancée.' Deliberately she whipped up her anger, using it as a shield against those other far more unnerving feelings she'd experienced, and heard him curse softly. He took hold of her arm, easing her between the couples dancing round the crowded floor to steer her towards a narrow glass door set into one wall. He pushed it open, pulling her through before closing it behind them and abruptly cutting off the sound of the music, the hum of voices.

Alex hesitated, then moved further into the room, looking round curiously at the lush display of vegetation. The air was very warm, filled with moisture and carrying with it the sweet aroma of damp soil as well as the perfume from the exotic blossoms.

Slowly, she followed the narrow path which wound between the beds of plants, stopping several times to examine a particularly spectacular specimen, aware that Jordan was following her. The path led to the centre of the conservatory, where

there was a wide stone bench set into an arch made
by the overhanging greenery, and she sat down,
resting her head back against the gritty, hard surface
as she watched him stop a few feet away. He drew
a packet of cigarettes from his pocket and lit one,
drawing deeply on it as he inhaled the smoke, his
face shuttered.

'You shouldn't smoke. It's bad for you.' Her
voice was low, in keeping with the quiet room, and
she saw him grimace as he shot a look at the
smouldering cigarette.

'I know. It's a loathsome habit, but not one I
give in to very often, I'm glad to say.' He took
another draw on the cigarette, then stubbed it out
and dropped the remains into a stone pot which
appeared to serve as an ashtray. 'However, I'm sure
we have more important things to discuss than my
bad habits. What did you think you were doing
before, telling people that I kidnapped you? You
could have caused no end of problems if they hadn't
thought it was some kind of a joke.'

Alex shrugged, looking away to focus on the
wide, smooth green leaves which almost touched
her head, terrified that he would somehow read
what she'd been feeling before in her eyes. What
was the matter with her tonight? She felt as though
her emotions were on a roller-coaster, swinging up
in one direction before dropping down in the other.
One minute she hated Jordan for what he was doing
to her, the next she felt these strange little flurries
of attraction when he touched her, as though she
had no control over herself any more.

Suddenly, he sighed, and came across to sit next
to her, stretching his long legs in front of him before

running a hand almost wearily over the thick darkness of his hair. 'Look, I know this isn't easy for either of us, but you'll achieve nothing by trying to fight me. This is the only acceptable way out of this mess you've created, and I'm not going to change my mind.'

'Acceptable? To whom? Maybe it's acceptable to you, but not to me! This isn't another one of your business deals. It's marriage! You know—to have and to hold, in sickness and in health, for richer, for poorer. Perhaps it doesn't bother you making a mockery out of it, but it bothers me!'

His face hardened. 'Oh, it bothers me all right. A lot, if you want the truth. You aren't the only one to have "finer" feelings, but I'm afraid we have little choice in the matter.'

'Of course we have a choice! Even if you won't believe that I am innocent, then surely you could find some other way to raise the money you need rather than go through with this crazy plan? There must be dozens of people willing to invest in a company as profitable as Lang's.'

Jordan shook his head, his expression bitter as he stared across the dimly lit bower. 'Don't you think I've already tried everything else?' He laughed harshly, no amusement in the sound. 'A couple of months back I had investors fighting to put money into the firm. I could have had any amount of cash I wanted, and any way I chose, but that's business for you—another roll of the dice and everything can change. Now you'd be amazed how many of those would-be investors are "unavailable" when I've tried to contact them! The word's out that Lang's is going through some rough water, and no one wants to get sucked in if we go under. The only way out is by using the money Mother left me, and as far as I'm concerned the company is far more important than the rights or wrongs of this marriage!'

'Then all I can say is that you are a fool.' Alex stood up, aching inside with a strange feeling of regret she didn't understand. 'You are willing to ruin both our lives to save the firm, but if you think I shall sit back and let you do it then you can think again!'

He came to his feet in one lithe motion, gripping her by the shoulders as he held her in front of him, his face dark with anger. 'Don't make the mistake of thinking I won't do everything I threatened I would do! I'll ruin you and your precious brother if you try to renege on our agreement!'

'I don't doubt you would!' Her eyes skimmed over him, bright with contempt. 'But one thing you haven't allowed for, Jordan Lang, is the fact that you would have to release me from the agreement if I proved my innocence. Isn't that so?'

'Perhaps. But from where I'm standing there is less chance of you doing that than of you catching moonbeams.'

Alex glared at him. 'Just you wait,' she said. 'I'll prove you wrong! All I want is your word that if I manage it you will drop this whole charade, and cancel all your plans for this...wedding!'

He hesitated, searching her face with a scrutiny that seemed to look right into her soul, then slowly he nodded, something akin to admiration softening his face. 'All right, then, yes; I give you my word that I shall release you completely from the agreement if you succeed in convincing me.' He smiled suddenly, letting go of her shoulders to brush a fist lightly across her jaw in a mock blow. 'You pack quite a punch when you set your mind to it. It makes me almost wish that we——'

He stopped abruptly, turning away to stride along the path towards the door, his back stiff. Alex drew in a ragged breath, forcing the painful pounding of her heart to slow as she followed him. What had he been about to say—that he wished that they could have met in different circumstances? She didn't know, but in her heart she knew that was what *she* wished. Given another time and another place, then could she and Jordan have established an entirely different kind of relationship? It was a tantalising and disturbing thought.

CHAPTER SIX

THE telephone rang just as Alex was getting out of the shower. Wrapping a towel round herself, she hurried to answer it, hoping it would be Kenny. She'd spent a restless night going over everything that had happened between her and Jordan—especially those last few minutes in the conservatory—and now she welcomed the chance to talk to Kenny to set herself back on even keel. Kenny had been against the plan from the moment she had explained it to him; it had been only after she had reassured him that she could cope with a few months of marriage better than with the alternative that he had agreed to go along with it. Now she needed that reassurance handing back to her to keep her on course.

Flicking a glance at the clock as she hurried into the living-room, she smiled as she picked up the phone, certain that no one but her brother would be calling at such an early hour of the morning.

'Hello. Am I glad you rang! You're just the person I need to talk to this morning.'

There was a happy anticipation in her voice, which faded abruptly when the caller spoke.

'Well, I never expected such a greeting! Does this mean you've had a change of heart, Alex?'

The smile faded and she stood up straighter, unconsciously tucking the towel more firmly across her breasts as though shielding herself against the shock.

'What do you want, Jordan?' she asked coldly.

'Do I have to *want* something? Isn't it only natural that a man should want to speak to his fiancée?' There were a host of nuances in his voice, and Alex felt her pulse skip a beat before racing wildly to catch up with itself. She drew in a slow breath, forcing herself to remember that this was Jordan she was speaking to—the man who was willing to blackmail her to get what he wanted; but it was strangely difficult to control the flurry of awareness those seductive tones evoked.

'I...I don't have the time to start playing silly games with you. Just tell me what you want and be done with it. I'm in a hurry.'

'You seemed eager enough to talk when you answered. Who were you expecting to be calling you?'

It would be so easy to tell him, easy and simple and sensible, but, for some perverse reason she didn't fully understand, Alex chose not to take the easy path.

'That is none of your business!'

'I disagree. I think it is my business! Don't forget that we have an agreement, lady, and there is no way I intend to let you jeopardise it!'

'What do you mean?'

'Just that I hope you realise that any...relationships you had are to be terminated immediately. I don't want any hint of scandal going about that my fiancée has been seen with other men! If there is anyone in your life, then get rid of him...now!'

It was an order, plain and simple and, as such, totally unpalatable. Alex reacted to it with instinct rather than logic.

'And what happens if I refuse?'

'Then you will regret it!'

'You don't own me, Jordan Lang!' she said furiously. 'I might have agreed to this plan of yours, but it doesn't give you the right to run my life and tell me what I can and cannot do!'

'You think not? Let's just get this straight here and now; nothing, and I mean *nothing*, is going to get in the way of this marriage! You will only be storing up more trouble for yourself if you push me by behaving stupidly. You are my fiancée, and that means ending any other relationships you have. I won't tolerate you making a laughing-stock out of me! However, I didn't ring up to have an argument with you.'

'No? Well, it seems you've succeeded anyway.' There was an icy sarcasm in Alex's voice, in complete contrast to the hot waves of fury racing through her at his domineering attitude. How dared he tell her how to behave? The fact that she wasn't involved in any 'relationship', as he put it, was by the way. She'd been too busy building up the business over the past couple of years to bother with anything more than casual friendships; but it angered her that he should take such a cavalier attitude, as though she was his property!

However, he ignored her tone and carried on as though she had never spoken, infuriating her more than ever. 'I rang to ask you to meet me for lunch today. There isn't much time before the wedding, and I think it would be better if people get used to seeing us together, to prevent too much speculation. I don't want any of our investors getting wind of the reasons why we are getting married in such a hurry. I suggest you meet me at the factory around one o'clock, and we'll go on from there.'

Alex snapped her lips together, her temper simmering. 'And what if it isn't convenient? I do have a business to run, remember?'

'I'm afraid what you want is of little consequence. Just meet me at one, or you will be sorry!'

'I hate you!' she said hoarsely.

'Do you?' There was a strange note in his voice as he asked the question—not anger, which she might have expected, nor even that cold mockery she'd come to dislike so much—and Alex felt a little shiver tingle its way down to her toes.

'You know I do,' she replied, trying her hardest to put as much conviction into the words; but he just laughed softly, a note of intimacy in the sound which ran along her veins like a bush fire, and sent the blood hissing hotly to her head.

'I thought you did, but I'm not so sure now that I've seen the photograph.'

'What photograph?' she demanded. 'What are you talking about?'

'You'll see. Just take a look at today's paper, Alex, and ask yourself if it really is hate...or something else?'

He cut the connection, leaving Alex staring blankly at the receiver until she dropped it abruptly on to its rest. She hurried into her bedroom, and slipped on a robe before running downstairs to collect the paper from behind the door. Frantically, she flicked through the pages, then stopped dead

when she came to the society column, her eyes
widening in gathering shock as she saw the photograph slap bang in the centre of the page. For one
incredulous minute she stared at it, then crumpled
the page and threw it on to the floor.

'No!' The cry echoed round the silence in the
flat, growing fainter and fainter so that she wanted
to scream it again and keep on screaming just to
make herself believe that it was true; but she had
the terrible feeling that it wouldn't be enough to
make it convincing. Bending, she picked up the
crumpled piece of paper, her hands shaking as she
smoothed it out and studied the picture once again.

It had been taken last night at the restaurant, and
showed her and Jordan together. Alex could remember the moment quite clearly, remember how
he had pulled her close to avoid another couple
dancing behind them, could remember how she had
let herself lean against him for that brief moment.
What she didn't remember was how she had been
looking at him, but the camera had caught her expression quite clearly, and she went cold to the
bottom of her heart as she saw the image of herself.
She had been looking at him at that moment not
with hatred in her eyes, but with the expression of
a woman in love!

'Mr Lang asked me to tell you that he's been de-
layed at a meeting, Miss Campbell. He shouldn't
be very long now. Would you like some coffee while
you're waiting for him?'

Alex smiled her thanks and accepted the cup of
coffee the secretary poured for her, carrying it over
to an arrangement of chairs grouped round a small

table near the window. Setting the cup down, she tried to relax, but it was impossible while her heart was beating so hard. What was she going to say to Jordan to explain that photograph? It was a question she had asked herself a thousand times that morning, yet she still had no idea what the answer was.

Picking up the cup, she took a tiny sip of the hot drink, then looked round the room, needing to focus her attention on something other than her own feelings. She caught the secretary's eye, and smiled self-consciously, glancing away as she set the cup back down again with a tiny clatter. It had been obvious from the moment she'd walked into the factory that everyone knew who she was and why she was there, thanks to that photograph and the accompanying article about the engagement. As she had made her way to Jordan's office, she had run the gauntlet of curious glances, the stifled murmur of comments. It seemed that everyone in the building was anxious to get a glimpse of the boss's future bride!

Her hands started to shake at the thought, and she clasped them together, willing herself to get a grip on herself. She couldn't afford to lose control now. She had to find the words to convince Jordan that what he had seen in that revealing photograph had been a mere trick of the light, nothing more, and definitely nothing as devastating as love! She *couldn't* be in love with a man who had done everything in his power to humiliate her and blackmail her!

The door opened, and she felt her heart lurch as she turned towards it, expecting to see Jordan, but it was James Morgan who walked into the room. He came over to her, once again subjecting her to that intent scrutiny, and immediately Alex felt her skin start to prickle.

'Miss Campbell, how nice to see you again so soon. How are you today? Recovered from all the excitement last night, I hope?'

'I'm fine, thank you, Mr Morgan,' she replied, fixing a smile to her lips as she met his searching gaze. 'It was a pleasant evening. I hope you enjoyed it?'

'I did indeed. I take it you have come to meet Jordan?'

'Yes. We're having lunch together.'

'Good. I must confess we were all taken by surprise when he announced the engagement out of the blue like that. It was all very sudden.' His eyes narrowed, as though he was testing for a reaction, and Alex felt a ripple of real unease work its way through her.

'These things sometimes happen like that,' she said non-committally, aware that the secretary was following every word.

'They must do. Strange, though—Jordan has always struck me as the sort of man who would never rush into anything without a lot of due thought.'

His tone was bland, the cool smile shaping his thin lips firmly in place, but to Alex's hypersensitive ears there seemed to be an underlying double meaning to the observation.

'I'm sure that anyone who works closely with Jordan would know that he would never take on a commitment unless he was a hundred per cent

certain that it was the right thing to do.' There was
a slight edge to Alex's voice, and she saw James
Morgan stiffen before he made an obvious effort
to relax.

'Of course. Forgive me if you thought I was im-
plying anything else. Everyone here has good reason
to appreciate his sterling qualities. Actually, that is
the real reason I popped in to the office. I wondered if you would like to have a look round and
meet some of the staff while you're waiting for him
to get back?'

'Well, I . . .' The last thing she felt like doing was
accompanying Morgan anywhere. He made her
uncomfortable. Yet it was hard to think of a valid
reason to refuse the offer.

'I'm sure Jordan won't mind you looking round.
He can't have anything he wants to keep secret from
his future wife, can he?'

There was no mistaking the challenge in Morgan's
voice, and once again Alex was struck by the feeling
that he knew a lot more about her situation than
he should. Suddenly, and for no explicable reason,
it became imperative that she should find out what
he knew.

'Thank you, Mr Morgan. I would enjoy that very
much.'

'Good.' He crossed the room and held the door
open for her, and slowly Alex walked through it,
feeling her heart thumping sickeningly fast in her
chest. Call it instinct, but something told her that
there was far more to this invitation than met the
eyes. She would have to be on her guard!

*   *   *

'And last, but not least, my office. The design centre of the whole factory, I think one can call it, where all the plans for our new projects are hatched. Have you ever been in here before? No, of course you haven't. Why on earth did I ask such a silly question?'

Morgan laughed hollowly as he unlocked the door and let Alex precede him into the room. It had been a whistle-stop tour of the factory, as they had rushed with almost indecent haste from one department to another, and Alex had the sudden unshakeable feeling that this room and what it contained had been the real reason behind his offer to show her round.

She looked round, her mind doing a swift hop backwards in time to that moment when the light had been flicked on and Jordan had confronted her. She drew in a ragged breath, forcing the disquieting memory from her mind while she coped with what was to come. James Morgan hadn't brought her here just to admire his office—he had to have a far more deadly reason that that.

'I thought you might be interested in seeing the blueprints for the new project we're launching soon. I'm sure Jordan must have told you about the problems we've had, but hopefully we're over those hurdles now.' He closed the office door and walked over to the safe, then hesitated and glanced at his watch. 'I'd better give Jordan's office a ring to let him know where you are, in case he's looking for you.'

He made the call, then smiled blandly at Alex, his pale eyes holding a hint of something which made apprehension rise in her chest. Suddenly, in the blink of an eye, she knew that the very last thing she wanted to do was to stay here in this room with him. She took a quick step backwards, then felt her legs turn to lead when he drew a familiar roll of pale blue paper out of the safe and spread it on the desk.

'Have you seen the plans before, Miss Campbell?'

His voice was low, oily, and she shuddered in revulsion. She swallowed down the taste of bile, wondering what game he was playing by asking that taunting question. She had no idea, but she had to keep her head until she found out.

'Should I have seen them, Mr Morgan?'

'No, of course not. I just thought that someone might have shown them to you.'

'I'm afraid there would be no point, as I'm sure I would never understand them.'

'Oh, they're not difficult to understand. An intelligent person would have no problems at all. Here, let me explain them to you.'

He stood aside, obviously meaning for her to join him behind the desk, but that was the last thing she was going to do!

'No!' She forced her voice down an octave or two, fighting the urge to turn tail and run from the room. 'Please don't trouble yourself. As I said, I've no idea how to read the plans, and no real inclination to learn. So if you'll——' She broke off as the buzzer on the intercom sounded, making her jump nervously. She drew in a deep breath while she tried to regain her composure, not bothering to listen to what Morgan was saying. All she was

interested in was getting out of this room and away
from those plans as fast as she could.

He switched the intercom off then smiled at Alex,
that cold little smile which never touched his eyes
and seemed to be more a mask than a true expression of his feelings. 'You will have to excuse
me for a few minutes, Miss Campbell. I'm needed
on the shop floor. Make yourself comfortable. I
won't be long.'

'Oh, but I'd prefer to go back to Jordan's office.
I'll find my own way.'

'Nonsense. We don't want you wandering round
on your own getting lost. I'll escort you back when
I'm finished.'

He had gone before Alex could protest any
further. She looked round, twisting the strap of her
bag nervously between her fingers, hating the
thought of remaining in that room until he came
back; yet she couldn't just walk out and leave the
blueprints lying around. They were too valuable—
as she knew to her cost—to take a chance on anything happening to them. It would be better to lock
them away in the safe and return the keys to Morgan
later.

She hurried round the desk and started to roll
them up, then looked up in relief when the door
opened, thinking it was Morgan coming back
already—only it wasn't him. Her heart lurched in
fear when she saw the expression on Jordan's face
as he saw her standing behind the desk with the
blueprints in her hands.

'What the hell are you doing?'

Maybe if he had asked her nicely she would have
told him, would have explained what had hap-

pened, step by careful step. But not when he adopted that accusing tone! She tossed the roll back on to the desk and faced him, colour flaring into her cheeks.

'What do you think?'

He closed the door and came further into the room, his grey eyes icy as he flicked a glance at the plans before looking back at her.

'How did you get hold of them this time?' There was a harsh bite to the words, an edge of steel that cut her to the quick, and Alex's head snapped back as though he had struck her.

'Would you believe me if I told you?'

'Damn you, woman! Don't you dare play games with me! How did you get those plans?'

There was a barely controlled violence in his voice, a tension to his body, which warned her he was on the verge of losing control. It frightened her into answering with a shade more caution.

'Mr Morgan left them on the desk when he went out of the office. I thought it would be safer if they were locked away before I left, and was just about to do it when you came in.'

'You really expect me to believe that? There is no way that James would be so careless as to leave them lying around! He's far too——' He broke off when the door opened and Morgan came into the room. The man stopped when he saw Jordan, his eyes running swiftly from one tense figure to the other, and Alex wondered if she was imagining the faint gleam of satisfaction which shone in his pale eyes.

'I'm sorry. I hope I'm not interrupting anything?'

'Of course not, James. Come in.' Obviously making an effort to control his temper, Jordan ran a hand round the back of his neck, kneading the tense muscles as he forced himself to appear relaxed. 'I just came to collect Alex, and was wondering what the plans were doing out of the safe.'

'Out of...? I could have sworn they were locked away when I left. Miss Campbell had asked to see them, but I'm almost certain that I hadn't got them out.'

There was a faintly puzzled expression on the older man's face as he glanced at the plans, and Alex stared at him in incredulity. What was he saying? He knew very well that he had left the plans lying around, so why was he telling all these lies? However, before she could challenge him, he picked them up and locked them carefully away. 'Good job it was Miss Campbell in here, though, wasn't it? I would have been for the high jump if it had been anyone else, but obviously our secrets are safe with her.'

Alex drew in a shaky breath, fighting against the hot surge of anger as she realised that it had been no accident. Morgan had deliberately left the blueprints out, knowing that Jordan would come to his office and find her with them! But why? What possible reason could he have for doing such a thing?

Her mind racing this way and that to solve the puzzle, she let Jordan lead her from the room, scarcely aware of what was happening until they stepped out into the car park. A cold, sleeting rain was falling, and she stopped to pull up her collar, but Jordan urged her on, seemingly oblivious to the heavy downpour which soaked them both in seconds. She glanced up at him, and something inside her seemed to shrivel up and die when she saw the expression on his face.

In total silence he led her to his car, barely giving her time to climb in before he slammed the door. It was quite obvious what he thought had been going on, and Alex knew that, no matter what, she had to convince him she hadn't been trying to steal the plans once more.

'It isn't what you think. I——'

'Why? Dammit, Alex, tell me! Why try it again? You're not stupid, but to attempt that in the middle of the day!' He swung round, his eyes burning into hers with a cold fire in their depths, and something else—something which made her stop and choose her words with care when pride demanded that she should answer just as hurtfully as he had. To see that fleeting shadow of regret on Jordan's face was something she had never expected to see.

'I didn't do anything,' she said quietly, willing him to hear the truth. 'It happened exactly as I explained. Morgan left the plans on his desk when he was called away. He was the one who insisted that I should see them, the one who took me to the office and got them out of the safe. I have no idea why he tried to make out otherwise. It was all a pack of lies.'

'Lies? Why should he want to lie to me? I've worked with the man for years, known him even longer. He was a part of Lang's when my father ran the company, so why should James start lying to me now? Why should he lie about you when he hardly knows you?'

'I don't know! I only wish I did. But it's the truth...all of it!'

'The truth? Hell, lady, you wouldn't know the truth if it got up and bit you! Your whole life is one huge pack of lies. I doubt if you even know what you're doing half the time.'

'No! You're wrong. Jordan, please! You must listen to me!' She caught hold of his hand, holding it tightly, willing him to open his mind to what she was saying. 'James Morgan was up to something today. He deliberately made it appear that I had asked to see those blueprints—but I hadn't!'

He shook her off, leaning forwards to start the engine with an angry roar. 'And you expect me to believe you after what's happened? I gave up believing in fairy stories a long time ago, Alex. But if you have any thoughts in your pretty head about taking what you know to your "friends", then forget them, or you will regret the day you ever heard of me and my company!'

'You can't threaten me like that, Jordan Lang!' she cried, willing herself to sound angry when inside she felt as though she was dying as she heard the contempt in his voice.

'I can do any damn thing I like, and don't you ever forget it. And number one on my list is bringing the wedding forwards.' He smiled, his eyes icy as they raked over her pale face. 'You should be flattered to learn I'm such an eager bridegroom. I'll arrange for a special licence this afternoon, so may I suggest that you go home now and start packing? You will be Mrs Jordan Lang within the week!'

'No! No, Jordan, you can't do this! I won't let you. I——' She stopped abruptly as he leaned over and pressed a finger lightly against her lips, damming the frantic flow of words.

'Yes, Alex,' he said softly, so softly that a shiver ran along her veins, trailing after the echo from the words. 'I'm calling all the shots now, and you will do exactly as I say or suffer the consequences!'

He drew back and set the car into gear, driving calmly out of the yard. Alex sat huddled in her seat, feeling the quaking spasm of fear racking her body as she realised she was beaten. No matter what she said or what she did, she would never make him change his mind now. But how could she face the next few months as his wife when he hated her so much?

CHAPTER SEVEN

MRS JORDAN LANG. The name sounded as unfamiliar as the weight of the gold band felt on her
finger. Alex stared at her reflection, studying the
pallor of her cheeks, the dull flatness of her eyes
as though she was seeing the face of a stranger.
That was how she felt—a stranger. No longer Alex
Campbell, but for the past hour Mrs Jordan Lang.
Someone entirely different.

The hotel-room door opened, and she swung
round, a faint colour stinging her cheeks as her
heart beat frantically; but it was only Kenny coming
looking for her. He shot her an anxious glance as
he closed the door on the hum of noise echoing up
from the reception area, then came and sat down
on a nearby chair. Alex turned back to the mirror,
picking up the brush to run it through her hair
again, needing something to keep her hands busy.

'Are you feeling all right? You look...' he
shrugged, unable to find the right words '...well,
different somehow.'

'I am different. I'm a married woman now, remember? Mrs Jordan Lang!' Her voice broke, and
she bit her lip to stem the sudden tide of hysteria
which threatened to crack the ice that had carried
her through the morning's ceremony at the register
office and the champagne reception afterwards,
held downstairs in this smart hotel.

Kenny swore softly, taking the brush from her hands as he turned her to face him. 'You don't have to go through with this any further, Lexie. He's got his piece of paper to claim his inheritance. There is no need for you to go and live in his house. Tell him to go to hell!'

Alex shook her head, her eyes swimming with unshed tears. 'I can't. It was all part of the agreement, and he won't let me get away with it. He'll want his very last ounce of flesh if I know him.' She covered Kenny's fingers with hers, hating to see him looking so worried. 'It will be all right. You'll see. Just a few months, and then we can put it all——' She broke off abruptly as the door opened and Jordan came into the room. His eyes narrowed when he saw Kenny, and immediately Alex let her hand slide away from her brother's and turned back to the mirror, watching Jordan coming closer through the glass.

'Are you nearly ready? People are waiting to wave us off.'

'I...' Her throat felt parched as a desert, her tongue swollen through a sudden lack of moisture, and she swallowed hard to ease the hot, gravelly feel of it. 'I'll only be a minute now. You go back down, and I'll be there as soon as I can.'

'I'll wait for you. It will look odd if I go back on my own, without my blushing bride—won't it?' There was cold sarcasm in his voice, and Kenny rose to his feet, twin spots of colour burning in his lean cheeks.

'Just be careful what you say, Lang. Or I'll——'

'You'll what? I don't think you are in any position to threaten me, Campbell.' Jordan didn't move, his face set as he met Kenny's anger with a cool, controlled contempt which only emphasised the difference between them—the fact that Kenny was no match for him in any circumstances. Kenny must have sensed it too because fury flashed into his eyes, and hastily Alex jumped to her feet and stepped in front of him.

'Stop it,' she ordered. 'This isn't going to get us anywhere. You go back downstairs, Kenny, and I'll be there in a minute.'

For a moment she thought he was going to ignore her. 'Please,' she said softly, catching hold of his arm and shaking it gently. 'I don't want there to be any trouble. I just want to get this over and done with as soon as possible.'

Kenny glanced at her, his expression softening. 'All right. But if you need me... And you, Lang, if you ever do anything to hurt her, then you'll have me to answer to!'

He left the room, leaving a wake of tension hanging in the air. Alex picked up the brush again and sat down, watching Jordan warily in the mirror. He had seemed strangely tense these last few days, as though there was something simmering just below the surface that was bothering him. Several times she had looked up to find him watching her with an expression on his face which she hadn't understood but which had made her feel uneasy. She had tried to refuse to see him until the day of the wedding, but he had overruled her protests with a heavy-handed determination, insisting that they must be seen in public together.

Now she could sense that same tension in him again, see that strange stillness to his features, as though he was thinking about something disturbing. The need to protect Kenny from anything he might be dreaming up was suddenly strong.

'Kenny was just trying to protect me, that's all. Obviously he's worried about this whole charade.'

Jordan didn't speak for a moment, staring into space until he seemed to gather himself. 'Then he's going about it the wrong way. It's about time he learned to control that temper of his before it gets him into any further trouble.'

'What do you expect him to do? Sit back nice and calmly while I'm press-ganged into this marriage? Obviously family loyalty is something you know little about!' Her tone was sharp, cutting through the tension hovering in the air, and Jordan's face tightened at the deliberate insult. Just for a moment he held her eyes in the mirror, then turned away to walk to the window, his hands pushed into the trousers of his dark grey suit, his wide shoulders rigid.

Alex drew in a shuddering little breath, knowing she was being foolish by needling him like this. She didn't want to promote any head-on confrontations. She wanted to let these next few months pass as quietly and emotionlessly as possible, because something inside her warned her she could be opening a Pandora's box by letting emotions run riot. She put down the brush and picked up a tube of lipstick in the same pale peach colour as her calf-length dress, outlining her lips with the glossy tint.

'Has it never occurred to you that you might be doing Kenny more harm than good by always jumping in to help him out of trouble?'

Jordan's voice was low, and Alex shot him a quick glance, feeling heat run through her when she saw that he was watching her. Nervously, she put down the lipstick, running a finger across the smooth wood of the dressing-table, feigning an intent concentration in its surface as she sought to avoid his eyes.

'I don't know what you mean. He's my brother; naturally I want to help him, just as he wants to help me.'

'But at some time in his life he has to learn to help himself. You can't keep mollycoddling him, Alex! He's gone from your parents to you, letting each of you make excuses for him rather than making him face up to his responsibilities!'

Is that what had happened? Had Kenny never learned to accept responsibility because he had always been overly loved? In a sudden flash, Alex knew it was the truth. She had taken on the role her mother had always performed, protecting Kenny rather than making him stand on his own two feet. Widowed at an early age, it had been natural that Janet Campbell should pour the love she'd felt for her husband on to the son who looked so like him. When she too had died ten years later, Alex had assumed that role and continued to shield Kenny from the realities of life. Now it was as if a veil had been torn aside by Jordan's observations.

She stood up, strangely unnerved by his astuteness, which left her feeling naked and vulnerable, as though he could read parts of her she didn't want him to read. Picking up the soft cream wool coat from the back of the chair, she started to shrug it on, jumping when he came and took it from her hands and slid it up her arms. Smoothing the soft wool across her shoulders, he turned her round, catching hold of the two wings of the collar as he held her in front of him.

'Would any of this have happened if it hadn't been for Kenny, Alex?'

His voice was low, washing through her like warm wine flowing through water, and she shivered, suddenly achingly aware of the touch of his fingers against her neck, the faint scent of his skin, the warmth of his body just inches from her own. Sensation flooded through her, bringing with it the memories she'd tried so hard to erase from her mind, memories of how it had felt to be held and kissed by him. Just for a moment the temptation to feel his kiss again was so strong that she took a half-step closer to him, then realised what she was doing. Self-contempt lanced her, and she drew away, her hands shaking as she buttoned the coat before looking up at him with a forced mockery in her eyes.

'My, my, Jordan; keep on like that and I'll start thinking that you've changed your mind about me and decided I'm innocent after all! And where would that leave this sham of a marriage?'

His face closed abruptly, the light dying from his eyes, leaving them dark and shadowed. He bent down and picked up her bag, handing it to her before opening the door. Alex walked past him, her head held high, wondering if it had been her overstrung imagination playing tricks. Just for a second there, before he had blanked it out, she could have sworn she'd seen guilt on his face; but of course she must have been mistaken. Jordan wasn't the kind of man who would ever feel guilty!

Jordan's house was set at the end of a short, tree-lined drive, a sprawling, oddly irregular building which had been added to at various times over the years, following the vagaries of its current owner. Alex had been prepared to dislike the house on sight, yet to her surprise she felt an immediate attraction to the place, finding nothing in its mellow red brick to resemble the stark prison her imagination had conjured up!

Stopping the car in front of the house, Jordan switched off the engine, then sat staring through the windscreen, his face still wearing that closed expression. He had said no more than half a dozen words since they'd left the reception, and Alex could feel her stomach lurching in anticipation of what was to come. She glanced down at her hand, unconsciously twisting the unfamiliar ring round and round her finger, watching the way the pale wintry sunlight reflected off its smooth golden surface. A wedding-ring should be a token of love and commitment, a golden promise of a future life together; yet all this ring was, was a symbol of Jordan's hatred for her. The thought was oddly bitter.

'Right, then. I suppose we'd better get inside and sort you out. There are a couple of things I need to get cleared up this afternoon, so I can't afford to waste any more time.'

Alex jumped when he spoke, colour ebbing and flowing in her cheeks when she glanced round and saw that he was watching her.

'I didn't realise you were going out,' she said to cover the confusion she felt, then silently cursed herself when she realised how it sounded.

He smiled, one dark brow raising slightly. 'I can always arrange to stay in if you prefer.'

Heat ran through her at the blatant suggestion in his voice, and she turned away, making a great show of gathering up her bag and the spray of orchids he'd pinned to her dress outside the register office. 'I don't care what you do,' she said snappily.

'No?'

'Of course not.' She swung the door open, then stopped when he caught her by the wrist, his long fingers locking firmly round its slender width.

' "Methinks the lady doth protest too much",' he quoted, his deep voice sending an unwanted *frisson* of heat scorching along her veins.

'Don't be ridiculous!' Alex forced a bite to the words, all too conscious of the feel of his hand on her arm. 'If you think I would welcome your company, then think again. I hate you, Jordan Lang, hate you for what you've done today, making me go through with this mockery of a marriage!'

'So you keep saying, but I can't help remembering that photograph.' He bent closer, his breath warm as it clouded on her skin. 'You didn't look as though you hated me then, Alex.'

'I...' Her throat closed, locking the denial deep inside. Ever since she'd seen that photograph in the paper she'd spent hours rehearsing what she would say to him if he ever mentioned it again, yet now she couldn't remember a single one of the dismissing little sentences she'd practised so carefully.

Helplessly, she watched his eyes darken as they dropped to her mouth. She knew he was going to kiss her then, knew to the depths of her soul that that was his intention, yet she couldn't seem to find the strength to stop him.

'No.' The protest was a mere token, dying on her lips as his mouth touched hers, his lips warm and gentle, so tender as they traced over hers that she felt tears spring to her eyes. Maybe if he had kissed her roughly, taken her mouth by force, she could have found it in her to fight him; but she wasn't proof against this gentlest of caresses.

'Alex.' Her name was a soft whisper of sound on his lips as he skimmed a shower of hot little kisses up the curve of her jaw to nibble delicately at the sensitive hollow behind her ear. Alex closed her eyes, letting herself drown in the exquisite sensations which made her body feel like liquid. His hand skimmed up her ribs, his fingers pausing briefly before they slid beneath the folds of her coat to curve lightly round her breast, teasing the nipple into aching tautness. Heat flooded through her, pouring along her veins, filling her whole body with a hot yearning.

'Jordan!' It was her turn now to whisper his name, her turn to skim kisses along the strong curve of his jaw, her turn to feel the shudders which rippled through him as she slid her hands over the hard muscles of his chest, feeling the crispness of hair beneath the thin silk of his shirt. He groaned softly, deep in his throat, and pulled her closer, pushing aside the soft enveloping folds of her coat so that he could press her against him and feel the desire-hardened nipples rubbing tantalisingly against his chest. Then slowly he put her from him, his hands rubbing lightly over the ends of her shoulders as he held her in front of him.

'Do you still claim to hate me so much, then, Alex?'

His voice was soft, but Alex flinched as though he had shouted the question. Her eyes flew open, and she stared up at him with horror in her eyes. How could she have done such a thing? How could she have forgotten who he was and why she was here, even for a moment? Great waves of shame ran through her, and she pulled away, opening the car door to climb out with the stiff, jerky movements of a person in the throes of shock. Hate and love: two opposing forces, or two sides of a single coin? She had no idea, but there was no way she was going to take any chances—not when this was just day one of six long months to be spent under Jordan's roof! She would be very careful from now on never to toss that coin in case it landed on the wrong side. To fall in love with Jordan would be the biggest mistake she could ever make in a relationship already memorable for its share of disasters!

She didn't want to go home, didn't want to go back and spend another evening making polite conversation. On the surface, she and Jordan seemed to be managing quite smoothly living together, but she'd become increasingly aware of the undercurrents which flowed between them. Was he aware of them too? He never gave any sign of being so, but

they had grown so strong in the past few days that
he would have to be blind not to be—and it
frightened her.

Three weeks hadn't dimmed the memory of how
easily she had responded to him that first day at
the house. When they were together, she was con-
stantly on her guard, and the strain was starting to
tell on her. If Kenny had been at home in the flat,
she would have locked the shop and gone upstairs
to talk to him for a couple of hours; but he had
decided to carry on working at the Yorkshire depot.
Alex knew it was the best thing for him; she'd
already noticed a subtle change in him when they
had spoken over the telephone—a hint that he was
finally growing up and accepting responsibility for
himself. Jordan had been right about that; he had
seen what Kenny needed quite clearly. Had he been
right about her too?

The thought shocked her, and abruptly she
chased it from her mind, looking round the shop
with haunted eyes before coming to a rapid, almost
desperate decision. She wouldn't go home. She
would catch a bus into Southport, and do some
late-night shopping. With Christmas only weeks
away, most of the stores would be open, and that
was just what she needed—the hustle and bustle to
take her mind off those fanciful ideas. Maybe she
would make a night of it—have a meal and take in
a show. It would give her a bit of much-needed
breathing-space.

It was later than she'd expected when she came
out of the theatre, having barely watched the
comedy show which had kept the rest of the
audience in fits of laughter. The warm, concealing

darkness had been just the place to nurture all those disturbing thoughts she'd wanted to weed out, and she was feeling more on edge than ever. She hurried to the bus stop and checked the timetable, her heart sinking when she realised she had missed the last bus through to Rainford. What on earth should she do now? She'd spent most of her money on a few presents and the meal and the theatre ticket, leaving just enough to cover her bus fare, but definitely not enough to pay for a taxi all that way.

Anxiously she glanced round, seeking inspiration, and spotted a bus turning the corner, its illuminated display showing its destination as Ormskirk. It seemed that fate had taken a hand in the evening, giving her the perfect excuse not to go back to the house at all. She would stay the night at the flat, and ring Jordan and tell him where she was.

She was aching with tiredness by the time she got back. She let herself in and switched on the central heating, then dialled Jordan's number. The line was engaged and she replaced the receiver with a definite feeling of relief. He wouldn't be very pleased about her staying here—not when he seemed so determined to foster the impression that theirs was the perfect marriage—but it was hard luck. There was no way she was going anywhere else tonight!

Humming to herself, she went into the bedroom to collect a short towelling robe from the wardrobe, then carried it through to the bathroom, and turned on the taps, filling the bath almost to the brim. Stripping off her clothes, she sank into the steamy heat and closed her eyes. She must have dozed off, because the next thing she knew was that someone was ringing the doorbell as though he or she was using it for bellringing practice, and the water was tepid.

Anxious to put a stop to the dreadful racket, she scrambled up, cursing loudly when a wave of water washed over the side and soaked the robe she'd left lying on the floor. Muttering evilly about what she would like to do to the demented campanologist, she dragged a towel off the rack and wound it around herself before hurrying to the top of the stairs. She hesitated, suddenly a shade uncertain about the wisdom of going down and opening the door, when another strident peeling spurred her into action.

'All right! All right! What do you want ringing like that? Who is it?' There was no doubting her displeasure from the tone of her voice, but it paled into insignificance compared to the answer which came roaring back through the door.

'Who the hell do you think it is? Now open this damned door!'

She gasped, her hand going to her throat to stem the wild pounding of her pulse. 'Jordan? Is that you?'

'Of course it is!'

Hands shaking, she fumbled with the lock, then stepped hurriedly backwards when he elbowed the door open and stepped inside the hall.

'What kind of a game do you think you're playing?' There was a dangerous glitter in his eyes as he rapped the question out, and Alex stepped back another pace, suddenly wary, then flinched when her bare shoulder-blades brushed against the coldness of the wall.

'Well, answer me, then! Where the hell have you been tonight?' He skimmed a glance over her body barely covered by the skimpy folds of the damp towel, and his expression altered subtly, taking on a harsh tautness of line which made a tremble of fear run down her spine. Reaching out, he caught her by the shoulders, his fingers biting deep into her flesh as he stared almost cruelly down into her face.

'Or maybe the question should have been, "Who have you been with tonight?"'

Alex gasped, twisting away, her own temper spiralling. How dared he come in here demanding answers and throwing accusations around? Suddenly all the pain and frustration she'd been bottling up for the past horrible weeks came bubbling up, and she rounded on him in fury. 'And what's it got to do with you?' She raised a mocking brow, her head tilted defiantly as she slid an insolent glance over his rigid figure. 'Where I've been and with whom has nothing to do with *you*, Jordan Lang!'

'No?' His voice dropped to a low purr, warm, silky, yet somehow far more disturbing than the previous anger had been; but Alex refused to let it throw her off course. She'd had enough, taken all she was prepared to take from this man. He had hurt her so many times over these past weeks with his cold comments, his deliberate refusal to believe anything she told him, and now all she wanted to do was to pay him back, hurt him as he had hurt her.

'No! I shall do exactly what I want and with whom I choose, and no one, especially not you, is going to stop me!'

'And you really think I'm going to let you? You think I'm going to sit back while you run around town making a laughing-stock out of me?'

'I can't see why it matters what I do. You've got your hands on the money now, so surely our "marriage" has achieved everything it was meant to do? I don't believe that your investors would care twopence if they found our marriage was on the rocks.' She laughed bitterly, sudden tears sparkling in her eyes. 'You've got what you want, Jordan, so what are you trying to tell me now—that you're jealous of the thought of me and another man? Or is it more a case of being a dog in the manger? You don't want me, but you sure as hell don't want anyone else to have me either!'

'Oh, I wouldn't say that, Alex.' He stepped forwards, not touching her as he stared down into her face, yet she could feel the imprint of his hard body hot against her own. Desperately she fought to keep her head, fought against the hot waves of longing which were filling her and threatening her sanity.

'Then what would you say?' she challenged, glaring up at him.

He smiled thinly, his eyes sliding over her flushed face and down the bare, slender column of her neck to stop at the shadowed hollow between her breasts in a slow, assessing sweep which Alex felt to the very heart of her being. She gasped, then felt the blood rush and eddy to her head when he reached out and trailed a finger lazily over the same path, letting it lie warmly just at the top curve of her breasts covered by the towel.

'I'd say that I want you very much, Alex, and that's the trouble. So maybe the sensible thing would be to do something about it!'

CHAPTER EIGHT

THE silence was something tangible, throbbing, pulsating, carrying with it a wild excitement that made Alex's breath catch in her throat. Helplessly she closed her eyes, giving herself up to the erotic images of her and Jordan together, then forced the pictures from her mind with a cold feeling of regret.

'No! No, Jordan, it wouldn't be sensible at all! It would be asking for trouble. I won't let this marriage become anything other than one of convenience!'

'I don't think you can stop it, Alex. I think it's way too late for that.' He bent and let his mouth trail over the bare curve of her shoulder, biting gently at the soft, warm flesh in a way that made a shudder race through her body. Slowly he drew back, his eyes glittering as he caught at the ends of the towel and eased the folds apart so that it fell to her feet, leaving her standing naked before him.

'No.' Her voice was a mere whisper of sound, uttering the denial yet carrying no conviction.

'Yes, Alex . . . yes!'

He swung her up into his arms, cradling her against him as he bent and took her mouth in a fierce kiss which burned the last attempts at protest from her lips. Alex whimpered softly, pushing her fingers into the cool hair at the back of his head, pulling his mouth down to hers so that she could

feel the hard lines of his male lips burning against
hers.

He carried her up the stairs like that—their
mouths locked so that his breath flowed between
her lips. Slowly he let her slide to the ground,
keeping her pressed against him so that she could
feel the abrasive rub of his clothing against her bare
skin sensitising every tiny nerve-ending until she felt
raw, on fire. His hands slid up her arms and stroked
across her shoulders, his thumbs tracing delicately
across her collar-bones in a rhythm which made the
blood drum in her veins. Her hands came up to
catch at his to stop the tormenting movement of
his fingers, but he just lifted them to his mouth and
ran his lips across her knuckles before setting them
back at her sides. He smiled slowly, his grey eyes
like satin as they slid up her body then came back
to hold hers as he forged a new, devastating path
down from her neck to the soft, ripe swell of her
breasts.

Alex caught her breath, feeling the dizziness of
heat flooding her limbs as his hands moulded gently
round the lush curves, testing the weight of her
breasts in his palms before sliding his fingertips just
once across the tightening buds of her nipples. She
cried out, her breath coming in short little spurts
as sensation gripped her, her hands lifting once
more to stop the tormenting touch of his fingers;
but once more he set them back at her sides.
Delicately his thumbs brushed across her nipples
time and again until they were rigid with a desire
she could feel echoed by the pulsing in the pit of
her stomach. Then, when she thought she could
stand the caresses not a moment longer, his hands

slid on, smoothing over her ribs and down over the soft curves of her belly before his fingers trailed a path into the silky curls between her thighs.

'Jordan!' His name was a cry of heaven mingled with the hot fires of hell as his fingers found the moist heart of her, stroking the hot flesh until her knees started to buckle under the force of an emotion she'd never known before.

He caught her to him, his hands sliding round to her buttocks as he dragged her against him, moving his hips against hers so that she could feel the hardness of his desire pressing against her. Taking her mouth, he kissed her hard, his tongue dancing with hers, mirroring the intimate movement of their bodies. When he drew back Alex moaned in protest, her eyes flying open, wide with the fear that he had just been playing with her again, using her as the butt for one of his cruel lessons; but he just shrugged off his jacket and dropped it on to the floor, studying her flushed face and the tousled beauty of her hair lying on her bare shoulders with an open satisfaction which sent little thrills shuddering through her.

Running his fingertips lightly down her arms again, he lifted her hands from her sides and laid them against his chest. 'Now you can touch, Alex,' he said softly, his eyes glittering as they stared straight into hers.

Just for a moment she hesitated, suddenly overcome by a strange shyness, until the hard warmth of the muscles under her hands and the steady pounding of his heart became too much of a temptation to resist. Delicately she eased the first button of his shirt open, then the next, her tongue caught between her teeth as she worked her way down the row with an intent concentration that was necessary when her whole body was trembling with tension.

Her hands slid inside the folds of soft cotton and ran lightly over the warm flesh, learning the contours until her fingers found the tiny rigid nub of his male nipple. He groaned, the sound low, deep, almost of agony as she stroked a finger over the very tip of it, then began to shudder violently when she pushed his shirt aside and pressed her lips to the ultra-sensitive spot, letting her tongue slide moistly over it time after time with an exquisite delicacy.

'Alex! Oh, Alex.'

Pushing his hands into her hair, Jordan dragged her head up, and took her mouth in a kiss meant to master, yet which ended up by giving more than it took. Alex gloried in the hot, wild pressure of his lips, the moist sweep of his tongue, the faint tremble she could feel racing through his body as he crushed her against him, gloried in the power she had over him. He could make her feel things she'd never felt before with any man, but she felt no shame, no embarrassment about letting him touch her and start these fires she could feel burning deep into her soul, because he felt the same.

His heart was beating just as wildly as hers, his strong body trembling with just the same fine edge of tension, his blood racing just as hotly through his veins as hers was racing. He was not seducing her... they were seducing each other, and the knowledge filled her with a sense of wonder.

When he bent and lifted her to carry her through
to the bedroom, Alex was with him heart and soul,
every step of the way, no thought of resisting lingering in her head. He laid her gently on the bed,
his lips skimming over the parted curve of hers in
a brief kiss which seemed to promise everything.
With the light filtering through the open bedroom
door, he undressed and came to lie beside her, his
eyes mirroring the passion she knew she could read
in hers. Alex smiled almost shyly at him, running
a hand up his chest to the strong line of his jaw,
feeling the faint rasp of stubble against her fingertips. He turned his head and pressed a kiss to
her palm, the tip of his tongue coming out to trace
a delicate pattern across the warm skin before he
laid her hand gently over the heavy pounding of
his heart.

'Have you slept with a man before, Alex?' His
voice was soft, his breath warmly sweet against her
face; yet Alex felt a cold shiver run through her,
carrying with it the sudden fear that he would no
longer want her when he heard the answer to his
question. Jordan was an experienced man, so would
he want to make love with an inexperienced little
virgin like her? She looked down, feeling tears
smarting her eyes as all her dreams started to
crumble into ashes.

'No. This will...this will be my first time.'

He went still, every line of his body tensing as
though he had received a blow, then slowly he relaxed again, lifting her chin with a gentle finger as
he stroked the tears off her face.

'Then tonight will be even more beautiful, more
special, for both of us.'

A fierce, wild elation soared through her, and
with a tiny cry she went into his arms, giving herself
to him with all the love she could feel in her heart.
Because, despite everything that had happened,
Alex knew that it wasn't hate she felt for this man,
but love—a wild, wonderful and powerful love!

Moonlight filtered through the window, drawing
the colour out of the familiar room, yet touching
it with a magical beauty in keeping with the mood.
Alex opened her eyes and looked round, her hand
sliding across the bed to touch Jordan; but the bed
was empty, the sheets cold. She sat up, her heart
beating wildly, then felt relief run through her when
she saw his clothes still lying on the floor. She lay
down again, letting her heartbeat steady while her
mind drifted back to the beauty of their love-
making. Jordan had promised it would be beautiful,
and it had been, so beautiful that it took on a
dreamlike quality, but it had been no dream. Every
glorious moment had been real.

She pushed back the rumpled sheets and got up,
looking round for a robe before picking Jordan's
shirt up from the floor and slipping it on. Just for
a moment she pressed the soft folds to her face,
breathing in the scent of him, which lingered on
the cloth, then smiled at her own foolishness and
buttoned it up. Barefooted, she made her way
through the flat, pausing in the doorway to the
living-room, her eyes locked on to the tall figure
standing by the window.

Dressed only in his suit-trousers, with his chest
bare and his dark hair lying in heavy disarray across
his forehead, he looked so vitally male that Alex

felt a thrill of possession ripple in hot waves through her. This man was her husband, hers to touch, to hold, to care for...to love. It no longer seemed to matter what had brought them together; those wonderful hours in his arms, when he had kissed and caressed every inch of her body, had given her the right to call him hers, just as she was now his, in mind as well as body. Nothing else mattered.

Silently she crossed the room and slid her arms round his waist, pressing her cheek against the bare, cool skin of his back. He started violently, the hard muscles under her cheek dancing before he relaxed and covered her linked hands with his, pressing her closer against him as though he couldn't bear the thought of her moving away.

'Penny for them,' she whispered, her lips feathering kisses against his skin.

He laughed, the sound rumbling under her ear, sending delicious tremors curling down to her toes. 'I don't think they're worth a penny!'

He turned round, sliding through the circle of her arms to link his hands behind her back and stare down into her upturned face. Alex met his gaze without trying to hide what he would see in her eyes. This was no longer a battle, no longer a game to score points and outmanoeuvre one another. It had gone way beyond that now. She loved him, and she wanted him to know it even if she couldn't yet find the courage to say the words aloud.

'Alex!' Her name was a litany, a prayer, as he bent his head and kissed her so sweetly, so tenderly that she felt her heart ache with the sheer wonder of it. She kissed him back, wanting him to feel the love she had for him, wanting to let it drift inside his heart and touch him to the very core just as it touched her.

He drew back slowly, pressing her head into the hollow of his shoulder, his fingers burrowed into the heavy weight of her hair. 'How did this happen, Alex?' There was a strange note in his voice which she didn't understand, and didn't want to. She drew back, seeing the harsh lines of strain etched on his face, the heavy darkness in his eyes, and felt fear run through her that he might be regretting what had happened.

'Are you sorry, Jordan?' she asked quietly. 'Because I'm not...not a bit sorry!'

'Aren't you?' There was a need for reassurance in the question, and she laughed softly in relief, snuggling back into his arms to press herself against the strong, clean line of his limbs.

'No, not a bit. Does that shock you?'

'Mmm, it does a bit.'

'Good! You deserve to be shocked out of your composure sometimes!'

'Oh, you've done that all right, and I don't just mean what happened between us before.' He pressed a kiss against her forehead, his lips warm, faintly possessive as they trailed across the smooth skin. 'You frightened the life out of me tonight, Alex, when you didn't come home. Where were you?' His arms tightened fractionally, pressing her closer to him as though trying to imprint the very feel of her on his skin. 'Were you with another man?'

She shook her head, feeling the slight relaxing of the punishing grip. 'No. I was on my own. There is no other man, Jordan.'

'Then where were you? When you didn't come home I thought you must have missed the bus, so I waited for a while, thinking you would phone. Then when I heard nothing I started to get worried. I came over to the shop and knocked on the door, but there was no sign of you, so I went back home, thinking you might have arrived and our paths hadn't crossed. It was only by chance that I decided to check the flat again before I called the police.'

'The police? I . . . well, I never thought you'd be worried.' She smiled sadly, unaware of how much of what she'd felt showed on her face. 'I knew you'd be angry that I hadn't come home, but it never occurred to me that you would be worried about me.'

He swore softly, lifting her chin to kiss her with a restrained savagery. 'Too damned right I was worried! I was almost out of my mind tonight when I couldn't find you.'

Alex gloried in the kiss, in the feeling of his lips imprinting their brand on hers. 'I'm sorry,' she whispered, running a hand gently down the side of his face. 'I just couldn't face coming back to the house tonight, so I went to Southport.'

Jordan sighed, running a hand caressingly down her back, his fingers trailing along the ridge of her spine before settling warmly in the small hollow at its base. 'Has it been so terrible, then?'

Alex shook her head. 'Not really, in the circumstances. It's just that . . .' She stopped, her face colouring delicately.

'Just what?'

'Just that there has been such an atmosphere these past few weeks. It felt as though we were living on the top of a volcano, waiting for it to explode. I couldn't face it tonight.'

'So instead you came here, and the volcano erupted just the same?' There was a wry note in his deep voice, and Alex smiled.

'Yes. I think you can definitely call it an eruption. Still, at least it's cleared the air.'

'Has it?'

'Of course it has!' She stopped abruptly, her whole body tensing on a sudden spasm of almost unbearable pain. She closed her eyes, fighting against the agony, wondering if she'd been the biggest fool in the world, and read more into what had happened tonight than he'd meant.

'What is it? Alex, answer me!' He shook her, forcing her head up as he studied her paper-white skin, but she wouldn't look at him, couldn't look at him until he'd allayed these vivid, dreadful fears.

'Do you still think I sold the information to your competitors?' Her voice was hollow, and she felt his hands clench on her shoulders so tightly that she knew she would have bruises later; but she welcomed the pain because it stopped the dizzying faintness from claiming her. Time seemed to stand still, holding them in the balance, ready to tip her from the warmth of euphoria into the cold depths of despair.

'Jordan?' Her voice was hoarse, raw with pain, and she felt him flinch as though she had struck him. Then, slowly, the biting grip on her shoulders eased, and he pulled her to him, cradling her against him, letting the warmth of his body seep into her cold flesh.

'No, Alex. I don't think you are guilty any more.'

The relief was so great that her knees buckled and she sagged in his arms, letting him take her weight. He swung her up, holding her so tightly that she could feel the heavy beating of his heart against her breast, feel the laboured draw of his breath. She opened her eyes then and looked up at him, seeing the pulsing nerve ticking along his jaw, mute testimony that she hadn't been the only one to suffer. She pressed her finger to the spot, feeling the steady tapping against her flesh, knowing that nothing in the world now had the power to hurt her. Jordan believed she was innocent!

Joy raced through her, and she turned her face to his, her eyes brimming with tears, wanting to give him something as wonderful as he had just given her. 'I lo——'

His head came down, and he took her mouth, stemming the words on her lips with a frenzied kiss that set her on fire, wanting him again just as much as she'd wanted him before.

It was only later, as she lay next to him in bed, her body languid with the aftermath of their love-making, that she wondered if there had been deliberation in the kiss. But why? Why should Jordan want to stop her telling him that she loved him?

CHAPTER NINE

IT WAS late when Alex woke up. For a few minutes she lay in bed stretching luxuriously, then she glanced at the clock and yelped in dismay when she realised how late it was. She jumped up, then paused for a second, letting her eyes linger on the rumpled pillow, which still bore the imprint of Jordan's head.

He had left a little after seven, kissing her long and hard before he'd gone home to change for a business meeting over at the Yorkshire factory. His eyes had held a hot desire as he'd lingered over the kiss, and Alex shuddered as she remembered it now, feeling the fires of passion igniting inside her again.

She had never imagined that love could feel like this—a deep, burning fire in her soul. If she'd thought of it at all, she'd imagined it to be something warm, soft, quiet, an emotion that grew slowly and gently, not this wild explosion which had rocked her off her feet. Loving Jordan promised to be just as devastating as hating him had been!

She laughed aloud at her own foolishness, and hurried to the bathroom, washing and dressing in record time before making herself toast and coffee and carrying it down to the shop. But no matter how hard she tried to concentrate on her work, her heart just wasn't in it. Finally, at a little after three o'clock, she admitted defeat, and closed up for the day. Last night the mere thought of going back to Jordan's house had scared her rigid; now she could hardly wait to get there even though she knew he would be late getting back. She wasn't silly enough to think that everything had been sorted out between them. There were still so many questions that needed answering—not least the one of exactly how he had come to decide that she was innocent. But that admission of his had been the turning point, giving her hope for their future together.

In a frenzy of anticipation, she caught the bus, sitting on the edge of her seat as it made its way to Rainford. Traffic was heavy at that time of the day, with the schools finishing, and they were held up for several minutes in the village; but at last they made it to her stop. Alex jumped off and almost ran along the road in her eagerness to get home just in case there had been a change of plans and Jordan had come home early.

It came as an unpleasant shock when she saw the car parked at the end of the drive and recognised the driver. She hesitated, then walked the last few yards to the door, forcing a smile to her lips as James Morgan climbed out and followed her.

'Hello, Mr Morgan. I'm afraid you've had a wasted journey if you're looking for Jordan. He's gone over to the Yorkshire factory; but surely you must already know about that? Did you come to leave him a message?' She hunted in her bag for the key, then felt the smile freeze on her lips when she looked up and saw the expression on his face.

A cold chill raced through her, stealing all the warmth from her limbs. It took every scrap of strength she possessed to ask the question she didn't want to ask.

'Has something happened ... to Jordan?' Her voice broke on his name, her face going ashen as the possibility that there had been an accident suddenly occurred to her.

'Not as far as I am aware, *Mrs Lang.*'

There was a faint mocking emphasis on her name, but Alex barely noticed it as relief ran through her in hot, sweet waves, making her go limp. It was several seconds before she realised that James Morgan was still talking.

'I'm sorry. I didn't catch that, Mr Morgan.' She smiled perfunctorily at him, slipping the key into the lock to open the door, wondering if she could get away without inviting him inside.

'I said that I haven't seen him today. I haven't seen him for several weeks, to be precise.'

'You haven't? I'm sorry, I don't think I understand what you are trying to tell me.' She withdrew the key from the lock, gripping it so tightly that the brass bit into her fingers. There was something about the calculating way that he was watching her, his pale eyes glittering with a suppressed excitement, that frightened Alex, though she couldn't have explained why.

'I'm quite sure you don't. I doubt if your *husband* has told you that he sacked me, let alone the reasons why.'

'Sacked you?' The fear had intensified, chilling her with its force so that she could only stand and stare at him with a growing apprehension.

'Yes. Don't you want to know why, Mrs Lang?' There was no mistaking the mockery now, no mistaking the hatred burning in those cold, flat eyes, and Alex drew in a ragged breath, fighting the feeling of panic.

'I don't think it has anything to do with me,' she said quickly, her voice shaking. 'If Jordan has seen fit to dismiss you, then I'm sure he had his reasons.'

'How very loyal you are! I wonder if you'll still feel the same when I tell you that he dismissed me for selling information about the new project to the firm's competitors? So you see it does have a lot to do with you, doesn't it?'

'You? You were behind it...but why? Why did you do such a thing?'

He laughed hollowly. 'Money, of course. Oh, and maybe the satisfaction I got from being able to pay Jordan back.' He stared at Alex, yet she had the feeling that he wasn't really seeing her; his thoughts were turned inwards, turning his face into an unpleasant mask of hatred.

'I've given that firm thirty-five years of my life, yet all I was due to receive when I retired was a pitiful pension and a handshake! That's it—for all the hard work I've put in, for being the brains behind most of their major projects...yet not once did old man Lang or his precious son ever acknowledge the fact and offer me a partnership!' His mouth twisted, his eyes glittering in a way that made Alex wonder if he was a little mad. However, he seemed to gather himself, running a hand over his thinning hair before continuing.

'I've been biding my time, but it wasn't until your brother came along that I realised just how easy it would be. I set him up, you see, left the plans out, knowing he would take them. He'd been waiting for a chance to get even after that dressing down he got. I made sure Jordan didn't fire him then— not when I had plans for him—but what I hadn't bargained for was your involvement. Still, in the end it turned out even better than I'd hoped.'

He laughed. 'I knew once I heard about the engagement what had happened—that Jordan thought you were behind it all. You had become the perfect scapegoat for me, and when you visited his office that day you played right into my hands. I'd needed an excuse to get hold of the modifications for my buyers, and there I had it. Perfect!'

'But it wasn't perfect! Jordan sacked you, so he must have found out that I was innocent!'

His face closed, an expression of cunning flashing into his eyes. 'I suppose he must, but no matter. I've still got enough to live comfortably on for a very long time to come.'

'But why are you telling me all this? Why did you come here today? Surely not just to let me know that Jordan thinks I'm innocent? I hate to disappoint you, Mr Morgan, but you've had a wasted journey if that's the reason. He told me himself last night that he knew now I wasn't behind any of it.'

'Did he indeed? And what else did he tell you, Mrs Lang? That he knew *before* the wedding, yet still chose to go ahead with it? Oh, I know all about his mother's will. It didn't take me long to work out that he was blackmailing you into the marriage so that he could get his hands on the money. He used you just as he and his father before him used me!'

Shock rippled through Alex, but she refused to show it, clinging on to the previous night's precious memories as a shield against what Morgan was saying. 'No! It wasn't like that! Maybe Jordan had found out I wasn't guilty before the wedding, but

he must have had other reasons for going ahead
with it.'

'What other reasons? You can't be foolish
enough to think he's in love with you? The only
thing that man loves is the business, and he would
do anything to protect it. He needed that money to
save the firm from bankruptcy, just as he needs the
rest of it to retain control of the company.'

'The rest? What are you talking about?'

'You don't know?' Morgan laughed harshly, and
Alex flinched, her whole body shaking with shock.
She had to hold on, had to hold tight to those
memories, which seemed to be slipping through her
fingers like sand. She closed her eyes, recalling the
way Jordan had held her last night, then felt the
image fade like smoke on the wind when James
Morgan continued.

'Jordan only received *half* of his inheritance on
his marriage. He will receive the other half on the
birth of his first child. I don't know what he's told
you, Mrs Lang, but he most definitely didn't marry
you for love! He married you to get his hands on
the money... every single tainted penny!'

Time slipped past, minutes and hours drifting away,
yet Alex was unaware of them passing as she sat
and waited. Her bag was packed, her coat neatly
folded over the back of a chair; all that was left
now was this final act, and then she could put
Jordan out of her life for good.

A car turned into the driveway, its headlights
sweeping over the windows, momentarily blinding
her; but she didn't move. She sat quite still, her
eyes blank, her heart empty, her body numb now
from the pain which had racked her since discov-

ering his duplicity. She had run the whole gamut of emotions that day, tumbling down from the dizzy heights of happiness to the black depths of despair. Now all she wanted was to get this last meeting over, and be free.

The front door opened and footsteps came along the hall, slowing as he must have seen her case standing outside the living-room. Abruptly he came into the room, switching on the lamps to flood the room with light, but nothing could penetrate the darkness in her soul.

'What's going on, Alex? Why is your case outside in the hall?'

She stood up to face him then, her eyes sweeping over the familiar planes of his face and body which her fingers had touched and caressed last night, and felt the pain swamp her again. Just for a moment, she closed her eyes as she fought to control it, then forced herself to look at him again. She had to look, had to remember every single detail of this man who had taken her life and crushed it into nothing.

'Dammit, Alex, tell me what's going on!'

He came towards her, reaching out to take her into his arms, but she wouldn't let him do that now, wouldn't let him work his treacherous magic on her again!

'Don't touch me!' She spat the order at him, her blue eyes burning in the stark pallor of her face, her hands clenched at her sides. There was a roaring in her head, a drumming in her ears as the blood surged round her cold limbs; but she ignored it, her whole being centred on the man who was watching her so intently. He stepped back, folding his arms across his chest as though to stop himself from reaching for her again, his face expressionless.

'What's happened?' His voice was deep, demanding answers, answers she had every intention of giving him. When she left here, she would do so knowing that he understood exactly why.

'I had a visitor today. He was waiting for me when I came back from the shop. I wonder if you can guess who it was, Jordan?'

'I hardly think this is the time for guessing-games. Why don't you just tell me what's eating you, and be done with it?' He loosened his tie and opened the top button of his shirt as he crossed the room to pour himself a measure of whisky. He cradled the glass in his hands for a second, swirling the rich amber liquid from side to side before swallowing it in one go and setting the glass down with a sharp clatter which made her jump. 'Well, Alex?'

He raised a mocking brow, his face falling into those familiar lines she'd learned to hate. It was as though last night had never happened, as though he had never held her, kissed her, felt her come alive in his arms. Had it really meant so little to him then? Could he now dismiss it so casually, just put it down to another of life's experiences? Or had it really been a deliberate attempt to fulfil the conditions of the will, to get her pregnant with the child who would ensure his inheritance and the safety of the company? Even though she had promised herself that she wouldn't let him hurt her again, it felt as though a knife had been plunged into her heart at the thought.

'James Morgan came to see me today. He told me that you had dismissed him for selling information about the new project. Is that true?'

'Yes.' His voice was curt. He sat down in one of the armchairs, crossing one long leg over the other before glancing coolly back at her. 'What else did he have to say?'

Would it have been easier if he'd sounded upset that she'd discovered what had happened, lost his composure even for the briefest moment? Alex didn't know, but the way he was able to sit there seemingly so unperturbed twisted that knife in her heart once more. She drew in a ragged breath, forcing herself to go on, to finish this business once and for all.

'He said that you knew before the wedding that I was innocent, yet you still went ahead with your plans. Why, Jordan? Why didn't you tell me? Damn you, Jordan, what right did you have to force me to go through with that sham of a wedding when you *knew* it was him?'

'What else could I have done?' He raised a mocking brow, his lips twisting into a bitterly wry smile. 'Would you have agreed to go ahead with the wedding if I had told you, Alex?'

'No...yes...I don't know! But you promised! You promised that you would cancel the arrangements if you had proof that it wasn't me!'

'How could I cancel?' He laughed harshly. 'You know why I needed to marry, Alex, and that hadn't changed!'

'So you were prepared to go ahead with it even knowing that I was completely innocent? My God, Jordan, is there anything you wouldn't do for your precious company?' There was scorn in her voice and on the flushed curves of her cheeks. 'I pity you, do you know that? The man with everything who really has nothing. You have no real idea what is important in life. All you can think about is that damned business, and everything else can go to pot!'

He got to his feet, his eyes burning into her like molten silver as he crossed the room. 'Damn you! Who are you to make judgements about me? What do you know about how I've struggled to get ahead of competitors, how I've worked to keep this company afloat?' He caught hold of her, ignoring her frantic struggles to get free. 'Lang's isn't some little two-bit concern. It's been in my family for years. It's part of me and, yes, I would do anything to stop it from being taken from me!'

Alex stilled, her eyes shimmering with unshed tears, feeling every word like a brand on her flesh. '"Anything"? Even going as far as getting me pregnant?' She laughed when he went suddenly still, his hands bruising her flesh, hysteria rolling inside her as she realised what a fool she'd been. 'Oh, yes, James Morgan told me about that too—a very minor detail that you must have overlooked! You're good, I'll give you that. You had me fooled into thinking that it was *me* you wanted last night, but it wasn't...not really. What you wanted was a child so that you could get your hands on the rest of your inheritance. You must have been laughing your head off when I fell into your arms! Would you have ever told me what you stood to gain, or would it have remained your little secret? After all, why should you need to tell me? Once I'd fulfilled your expectations, then it would be easy enough to get rid of me!'

'Stop it!' He shook her so that her head rolled, then caught hold of her chin, forcing her face up. 'You're getting hysterical.'

'Am I? Well, fancy that. Silly of me, getting hysterical because I've just found out that I've been duped!' Her breath caught on a sob, and she looked up at him with haunted eyes, wanting even then to hear it wasn't true, and salvage just one of her shattered dreams. 'Was Morgan telling the truth, Jordan? Do you stand to inherit more money if...if you have a child?'

'Yes! Yes, it is true; but last night wasn't for that!'

'And you really expect me to believe you, after all the lies, all the deceit? If it weren't for the sake of acquiring a child, then what was it for? The novelty value of sleeping with a virgin, or just a way to satisfy your lust? Neither of them are very attractive, are they?' She tossed her hair back from her flushed face, smiling tauntingly, hurting inside so much, and wanting at that moment to hurt him back in the only way she knew she could. 'Well, hard luck, because there won't ever be a child. I shall make certain of that!'

'And what exactly do you mean by that?' There was a dangerous edge to his voice, but Alex chose to ignore it, too far beyond the bounds of caution to care.

'What do you think? No woman needs to have a child she doesn't want nowadays, and I don't want yours!'

'You'd have an abortion?' There was a strange note in his voice, but she didn't hear it, deaf to anything but her own pain and the desire to hurt.

'Yes! There will be no child from this marriage...believe me!'

'I wouldn't let you do it! Damn you, Alex, you have no idea what you're saying at the moment,

but if there is to be a child then there is no way that
I would let you kill it just to get back at me!'

'There is no way you will be able to stop me!'
She pulled away from him, evading his hands as he
tried to catch hold of her again. Sweeping up her
coat from the back of the chair, she shot him an
anguish-filled look, aware that her control was
liable to snap at any moment. 'I'm leaving you,
and I don't want to have anything more to do with
you from this moment on!'

She walked towards the door, then gasped when
he swung her round, his hands pinning her in front
of him as he glared down into her white face.

'No! I'm not letting you leave here, not tonight
or any other night. We had an agreement, and I
intend to see that you stand by it!'

'Agreement? You have the gall to remind me of
that after what you've done, the way you've tricked
me, used me? It's over, Jordan. From now on any
agreement we had is terminated!'

'No! I'll make you stay.'

'How? Surely you're not going to resort to the
tactics I once accused you of planning?' She
laughed into his face, feeling the bitter tears welling
in her throat. 'Do you really think you can keep
me locked up for the rest of my days?'

'Who said anything about locking you up?' His
gaze slid to her mouth, his hands softening as he
slid them up from her arms to curl around the
slender column of her throat while he caressed the
sensitive flesh, his fingers tracing gently, seductively round behind her ears and into the warm mass
of her hair lying on the nape of her neck. 'Would
I really need to lock you up, Alex? Or could I just

achieve the same outcome by a much more pleasant method?'

'No! No, Jordan, I don't want——'

The words were lost as he lowered his head and took her mouth, his lips hard and bruising, forcing hers apart so that he could slide his tongue inside her mouth to run hotly round the softly sensitive contours. Alex fought him, turning her head from side to side as she tried to break the contact, but he wrapped the length of her hair round his hand and held her still. Determinedly, he deepened the kiss, running his hand down the column of her neck to slide inside the neck of her blouse and caress the soft curves of her breasts.

Alex whimpered, fighting against the sensations which were even now racing through her body, carrying with them the hot surge of memories from the night before. It would be so easy to let him kiss her, love her, make her forget what he had done; but deep in her heart she knew it would never be enough. He had tricked her, used her body, and what he could make her feel, against her, in the most cruelly destructive way possible. Even though she knew she loved him, she could never forget what he had done.

She raised her hands, catching him off guard as she pushed him roughly from her. She stood and faced him, panting slightly, her mouth red and bruised, her eyes brimming with tears.

'No! I won't let you do it again, Jordan. I've been a fool too many times, but no more. I'm leaving you, and that's it...final!'

'I can still ruin you!'

She looked at him with scorn, feeling the last of those foolish dreams shatter beyond repair. 'Do what you like, but just remember one thing: I was never guilty! You accused me of stealing that information, and refused to listen when I told you it wasn't *me*. The only thing I am guilty of is being foolish enough to let you do it!' She smiled bitterly. 'I should have called your bluff right from the beginning, told you to do your worst, because nothing could have been as bad as what you have done!'

She swung round and walked to the door, her hand trembling as she turned the handle.

'And what if there is a child, Alex?'

His voice was low yet holding a note which made her stop when all she wanted was to get away before her heart broke completely. She glanced back, her eyes lingering for one last time on his tall figure, the lean planes of his face she could have drawn from memory, and the tears she'd held in check started to slide silently down her face.

'That is something you will never know,' she whispered hoarsely. She ran from the room, hearing him shout her name, but she didn't stop, didn't even turn to look back. It was over, everything which had started in anger had ended in this dreadful anguish. She never wanted to see Jordan Lang again.

CHAPTER TEN

ALEX wasn't pregnant.

Even though she knew she should be glad not to add that to all the other problems she faced, she couldn't help the overwhelming sense of loss she felt when she discovered the fact. In her heart she knew that, although she had taunted Jordan with the claim that she would have an abortion, she would never have gone through with it. Now the fact that there would be no child was yet another wound in her aching heart.

Jordan had made no attempt to contact her in the weeks since she'd left him, but that hadn't changed how she felt about him; she wished it had. No matter how hard she tried to flip the coin again and find hate in her heart, all she felt was this love, which was slowly tearing her apart. On the surface she appeared to be handling their break-up with a cool detachment, but underneath she was hurting with a pain which went beyond words.

Even Kenny had no real idea how she felt. He had greeted the news that Alex was no longer living in Jordan's house, and that their agreement was terminated, with curiosity mingled with open relief. Alex had given him some kind of an explanation, swearing him to secrecy when it became obvious that the real reason for James Morgan's sudden disappearance from the company hadn't become public knowledge, but she hadn't been able to find the courage to tell him what had happened between

her and Jordan. That was something too personal
to share with anyone, even Kenny.

The time passed slowly. Alex filled the days by
working in the shop, then carried on way into the
early hours crafting her jewellery, hoping to tire
herself enough to sleep. But, no matter how
exhausted she was, sleep was fitful, broken by the
vivid dreams which brought her awake with tears
drying on her cheeks. She could only hope that arrangements would be made to end the marriage
soon. Maybe then she could get on with the task
of living again.

A few days before Christmas she was tidying the
display cases prior to locking up the shop for the
day. It had been a busy afternoon, with people
rushing in to buy last-minute presents, and she was
already thinking longingly of going upstairs to enjoy
some peace and quiet after all the rush. She bent
down to lock the bottom of the case, then groaned
under her breath when she heard the shop bell
tinkle, announcing yet another customer. Fixing a
polite smile to her lips, she straightened then felt
her heart flutter to a halt when she saw Jordan
standing in the doorway.

'Hello, Alex. How are you?'

His voice was just as she remembered it, just as
she heard it every night in her dreams, making her
tremble with the memories it evoked. Just for a
moment they came flooding back in a hot tide
before ruthlessly she drove them from her mind.

'What do you want?'

He stiffened at the curtness of her response, his
body going rigid, his face all stark bones and angles.
Dressed in a heavy black leather jacket and dark
trousers, he cut a sombre figure, and Alex felt

unease work its way coldly down her spine. She bent down to finish locking the case to give herself a moment's breathing-space to recover from the shock of his unexpected appearance, then stood up, gripping the edge of the counter so hard that her fingers throbbed from the pressure.

'Well, Jordan? I haven't got all evening to waste. I was just about to close up for the night so, if you have something to say, please get on with it.'

Colour ran along his cheekbones in an angry tide, and he moved closer so that Alex could smell the familiar scent of his skin mingled with the faint tang of his aftershave—a heady aroma which she remembered so well.

'You appear to be in something of a hurry. Are you going somewhere special?'

There was a faint edge to the question which she took immediate exception to. She raised a mocking brow, her head tilted at a regal angle. 'I might be, but frankly I fail to see what business it is of yours!' She smiled faintly, somewhat mollified to see the anger flicker in his eyes as the jab struck home. 'Now, I assume you do have a reason for coming here?'

He shrugged, glancing down at the display case with its glittering treasure of gold and jewels. 'I might just have come to buy something. There are one or two presents I still need to get.'

For whom? Alex bit her lip to stop the question from rushing out, feeling sickness welling in her stomach at the thought of Jordan buying presents for another woman. How was it that every time she struck out at him it ended up being such a feeble blow, one he could deflect and turn back on her? Now all those vivid dreams would be twice as awful, featuring some faceless woman who had a claim on him.

Terrified that he would sense how she was feeling, she rushed into speech. 'I've already locked everything away for the night, so I'm afraid you will have to go elsewhere to do your shopping.'

He smiled thinly, his eyes meeting hers and holding them. 'Business must be doing well if you can refuse a sale out of hand like that!' He looked into the glass case, studying the display with apparent interest. 'I rather like that ring—the emerald one. How much is it?'

She would rather starve first before she sold him some of her jewellery... to give to another woman! 'It's not for sale.'

'No? Then how about the sapphire and diamond cluster next to it?'

'Neither is that. None of them is for sale... to you!'

'I see. Well, it seems a strange way to run a business, Alex—letting your heart rule your head.'

There was a trace of knowing mockery in his voice, and she flushed. She forced herself to face him, hating the fact that he had realised just how vulnerable she was. 'I'm sure that is something you *never* have a problem with. I can't imagine you ever letting emotion take precedence over business matters!'

His face tightened, the mockery fading, leaving his eyes like shards of cold steel. 'What do you expect, Alex—that I should apologise for what happened?'

'I expect nothing from you... nothing at all! Now, if you haven't anything else to say, then I'd be glad if you'd leave.'

'Oh, I've plenty to say all right. There's a lot we need to talk about.'

'Such as? Just tell me one thing we have to——' She stopped abruptly, her face losing all its colour as she suddenly realised why he'd come. 'Aren't I stupid? I should have realised what you wanted.' Her voice was hoarse, empty, drained of all emotion—even anger—now. 'I hate to disappoint you, Jordan, but your plan failed; I'm not pregnant!'

'That isn't why I came. Dammit, Alex, can't you ever give me the benefit of the doubt?'

'The same as you gave me? You taught me well, Jordan Lang, taught me to be suspicious of even the simplest action—so you only have yourself to blame. But now that you have what you came for, I think you had better leave.'

'I'm not going anywhere until you stop all this foolishness, and listen to me.' He glanced round the empty shop, rough impatience in his voice. 'For heaven's sake lock up, and let's go up to the flat. All I ask is that you give me ten minutes of your time.'

'I haven't got ten minutes to spare for *you*. Now get out!'

'And if I refuse? What will you do then, Alex? Eject me bodily?' He slid a glance over her slender figure, then folded his arms complacently across his chest. 'Somehow I don't think you're up to a physical confrontation, but be my guest if you want to try. You never know, sweetheart, we might both enjoy it!'

Fury ripped through her at his total arrogance. He needed taking down a peg or two, and she was just the woman to do it!

'You think not?' she asked sweetly, moving slowly further along the counter until she could feel the coldness of the button beneath her searching fingers. 'I shall ask you just one last time, Jordan. Will you please leave?'

'No.'

'Then you only have yourself to blame!' She pushed the button in, jumping even though she knew what was going to happen when an ear-splitting noise rent the air.

'What the hell . . .?'

'The panic alarm.' She had to shout so that he could hear her over the sound, her blue eyes filled with triumph. 'It's linked in to the police station, so I suggest you leave pretty sharply if you don't want to spend the next couple of hours making a statement to them when they arrive!'

'Why you little——!' He broke off, and swung round on his heel to stride towards the door and wrench it open. Just for a moment he paused and shot a glance over his shoulder at Alex, who was standing by the counter with her hands pressed tightly over her ears, then walked out, slamming the door behind him.

Alex drew in a shaky breath, then ran round the counter and locked the door before hurrying through to the back to ring the police station and cancel the alarm call. It took her three attempts to dial the number successfully because her hands were shaking so hard. She might have won that round but, remembering that last look Jordan had given her before he'd left, she had the uncomfortable feeling that she hadn't won the whole game!

He would be back!

Even while she threw clothes into a suitcase, Alex

knew that it was a race against time. How long had it been since he'd left? She glanced at the clock, trying to work out how much time had elapsed, but her brain was still too hazy with fear to cope with even the simplest of arithmetic. All she knew was that Jordan would be back, and that she mustn't be here when he arrived!

With a gasp of relief she managed to close the case, and hefted it off the bed before snatching up her bag to check she had some money in her purse. If she could find a taxi, she should be able to catch the last train through to York. She would ring Kenny from the station and tell him to collect her.

She hurried downstairs, dropping her case by her feet while she locked up, then buttoned her coat against the cold chill of the night air. Although it was barely six o'clock, the sky was inky dark, heavy clouds blotting out any traces of moonlight, and promising another downpour of rain at any minute. She could only hope that she would be able to pick up a taxi before it started.

'Going somewhere?'

She swung round at the sound of his voice, her face going paper-white as she saw him leaning almost indolently against the wall. For one dreadful moment she stood rooted to the spot, then suddenly came to her senses. Scrabbling frantically in her pocket for the key, she turned to go back inside, but she never even got the chance to put it in the lock before Jordan was beside her, his hand fastening firmly round her arm.

'Oh, no, you don't! You're not getting away from me this time!'

'Let me go!' she ordered shrilly, twisting her arm, but his fingers fastened even more firmly, his mouth curved into a grim little smile as he watched her frantic struggles.

'No chance. You've done all the running you're going to do. Now you're coming with me.'

He picked up her case and pulled her with him as he hurried down the street almost before she had a chance to realise what was happening. She stopped dead, her eyes flashing with anger, her breath coming in short, furious spurts.

'Stop it! What do you think you're doing? Where are you taking me?'

'You'll see.'

'I don't want to "see". I'm not going anywhere with you—not tonight or any other night! Now let...me...go!'

She wrenched her arm away from him, somewhat surprised when he didn't try to stop her this time, but just stood and watched her. Her eyes narrowed thoughtfully as she wondered what kind of a game he was playing, but it was impossible to tell from the expression on his face. 'What do you want, Jordan? Why have you come back? I thought I made it perfectly plain before that you are not welcome.'

He didn't like that; Alex could tell from the flicker in the depths of his eyes, the way his jaw stiffened, but, surprisingly, he spoke quite calmly. 'Just a chance to talk to you, as I said before. That's all I'm after.'

'And, as I told *you* before, there is nothing to talk about! The only thing left to talk about is the divorce, and I don't see that will cause any major problems.' She smiled bitterly, pushing the tumble of hair back from her cheeks. 'I imagine that was all fitted into your plan, wasn't it? All neatly numbered?'

'I didn't come to talk about any divorce.' He glanced round impatiently at the heavy traffic. 'Look, this isn't the place to have a conversation. Come back to the house with me, and let's see if we can't straighten this mess out.'

'No!' She stepped back, her face going pale at the thought of going back to his house with him. She couldn't bear it, couldn't bear to go there again when that last dreadful confrontation was still so raw in her mind. She loved him, but she wouldn't let him hurt her again as he had hurt her before. 'It's far too late to sort anything out. The damage has been done now, and all that is left is for us to end this stupid sham of a marriage and go our separate ways.'

'No!' He caught her arm, pulling her back towards him, his eyes burning into hers with a silver fire in their depths. 'It's not too late, Alex. I won't let it be!'

The arrogance of the assertion took her breath away. 'You won't let it be? Just who do you think you are, Jordan Lang?' She laughed harshly, her eyes brimming with tears, so that she didn't see how he flinched, how every bone in his face stood out in stark relief. 'What gives you the right to decide other people's lives? Who said you could play God and decide my life because it suited you? I hate you, do you hear me? I hate you for what you've done to me!'

Her voice broke on a sob, and she bent her head, feeling the futility of it all wash through her, too upset to resist when he drew her into his arms. Cradling her shuddering body against him, Jordan stroked her hair, and Alex was surprised to feel how his hand trembled.

'Don't, Alex,' he ordered softly, a wealth of pain in his deep voice. 'You know it isn't true. You're upset, but you don't hate me.'

'I do... I do!'

He bent and kissed her then, not fiercely as a punishment for her defiance, but so gently, so tenderly that it made her heart ache afresh for all that she had lost. Slowly he drew back, cupping her face between his hands as he brushed a shower of soft, fleeting kisses over her mouth and the damp curves of her cheeks before tilting her head up to meet his steady gaze.

'You don't hate me, Alex, although you should for what I've done to you. You love me.'

'No!' Even while her lips framed the denial her eyes betrayed her, tangling with his with a blaze of love burning in their depths that he would have had to be blind not to see. He sucked in a ragged breath, his lips rimmed with white as he struggled for control, his hands tightening convulsively against her face.

Terrified by the way she had given herself away, Alex stumbled into speech. 'No. You've got it all wrong! I don't——'

He pressed his fingers against her mouth. 'No, Alex. Don't lie to me. You love me. I knew it the other night when we made love. You would never have given yourself to me otherwise, would you?' He shook her gently, but she refused to look at him, her world and her pride lying in ruins around her feet. 'What we shared wasn't just sex. It went way beyond that for both of us, and I won't let you try and cheapen it now by lying.'

What was he trying to say? That he loved her? For one glorious moment Alex's heart lifted and soared to the heights before spinning sickeningly back to the depths. How could she ever believe anything he said after what he'd done, the way he had tricked her?

'No!' She tried to pull away, to free herself from the touch of his hands, which was ripping her heart into shreds; but he wouldn't let her go this time. 'Don't do this, Jordan,' she begged brokenly. 'Please don't do this on top of everything else.'

He swore roughly, sliding his hands down her arms to grip her wrists so hard that she winced from the pain, yet she knew he was unaware of what he was doing. 'I am trying to tell you that I love you, Alex. I know it's hard to believe. Lord knows, I've been finding it hard to come to terms with myself; but I do! All I ask is that you give me a chance to convince you that I'm telling the truth. Don't destroy both our lives because you're afraid!' He let her go so abruptly that she staggered, pushing his hands deep into the pockets of his jacket. 'Will you come with me, Alex? I can't make you. I promise I won't even try. All I ask is that you give me this one last chance, and if you don't believe me I will step out of your life for good.'

For a moment which bordered on eternity, Alex hesitated, terrified of making the wrong decision and of being hurt again as she'd been hurt before; and Jordan misread that hesitation as refusal. His face closed up and he turned quickly away, walking off down the street with his head bowed.

Alex stood and watched him go, feeling the pain rip through her once again as she realised he was walking out of her life for good.

'Don't go.'

The wind caught her whispered plea and carried it away, swirling it up into the sky, too faint for him to hear. He kept on walking, his long legs setting more and more distance between them, and suddenly Alex knew she couldn't let it end like this. If there was even the faintest hope that he was telling the truth, then she had to take it.

'Jordan!' She screamed his name, terrified that he wouldn't hear her and keep on walking, but he stopped as though he'd been struck. Slowly he turned to face her. Alex took one small hesitant step towards him, then another, then, with a choked sob, ran down the street and hurled herself into his waiting arms.

They drove in silence, a silence Alex was afraid to break. Who was it who had said that it was better to journey than to arrive? She couldn't remember, yet it summed up how she was feeling so exactly. While they were travelling along the roads like this she could keep the hope alive that he had been telling her the truth. She didn't think she could bear it if she found out it had all been lies and still more trickery at the end of the journey.

Jordan swung the car off the road, and drew to a halt, cutting the engine to leave them in a silence which hummed with tension generated by so many unanswered questions. Alex drew in a shaky breath, forcing herself to look round while she tried to gather her composure for what was to come, and realised that they were parked at Ashurst Beacon. Below them, where the hill fell away, she could see the lights of Skelmersdale like rows of glittering jewels shining against the black velvet of the night sky. So many people down there, so many lives running along familiar lines, yet up here the next few minutes would decide her fate. Suddenly she couldn't bear the waiting a minute longer.

'Jordan, I...'

'Alex...'

They spoke together and stopped. Slowly, Jordan reached out and pushed a long strand of hair off her face, his fingers trembling slightly as they brushed against the softness of her cheek, and that evidence of nervousness said more than any amount of words could ever have done. To know that Jordan, who had always been so assured and in control before, could shake like this, seemed to ease the tightness of fear which had gripped her ever since she'd got into the car.

She caught his hand, linking her fingers with his as she drew it on to her lap, her eyes soft and gentle as she looked back at him.

'Do you really love me, Jordan?'

'Yes, Alex, I really do. I know it's asking a lot of you to believe me after everything that's happened—but I love you.'

There was no doubting the sincerity in his voice, and Alex felt a wave of happiness race through her. But she had to contain it at least for a little while until everything had been brought out into the open and all the questions had been answered. If they were to build a future together, there could be no room in it for lies—only truth.

'Do you think you can explain everything to me?'

He nodded, lifting her hand up to his lips before letting it go and turning away to stare out through the windscreen, as though what he had to say was going to be painful. 'You have to understand, Alex, that for the whole of my life Lang's has been the most important thing in it. I was brought up on the idea that ensuring its well-being was the only thing that mattered.' He shrugged, a fleeting sadness on his face as he glanced at her. 'My parents divorced when I was twelve, and after that my father immersed himself in the business to the exclusion of everything else. Lang's was his whole life, the only comfort he had in a lonely existence. Keeping it going and ensuring that it flourished was my way of paying tribute to him. Can you understand that?'

'I think so...yes, I can. But surely your desire to keep the company safe didn't merit the drastic measures you took?'

'I'm afraid it did. There was too much sunk into this project for the company to recover if it failed. I needed that money Mother left me; let's make no bones about that!'

'But was it true about the rest of it?' Alex's face clouded, her eyes dim with pain. 'Did you sleep with me to get me pregnant so you could inherit the rest of the money?'

'No!' Jordan caught her hands, holding them firmly. 'I slept with you because I couldn't stop myself that night! I wanted you so much that I was helpless to do anything else.' He laughed wryly, bending to brush a light kiss over her mouth, leaving a trail of fire behind to linger tantalisingly on her lips. 'You had me well and truly in your clutches by then, lady, although I would have denied it if you'd asked me! I knew I was attracted to you right from the start. That's one of the reasons why I was so angry about what I thought you'd done, and went to such lengths to find you. I don't think I would have come up with this marriage plan if I hadn't been, though I was blind to that fact until it was too late!

'There was no way I could have stopped myself making love to you when I came to the flat and found you looking like something out of one of my more erotic dreams. The thought of a child and the rest of the money definitely didn't enter my head!'

'I'm glad,' Alex whispered shakily. 'You were right, of course. I would never have slept with you if I hadn't been in love with you. And later, when you told me that you knew I was innocent—well, I can't explain how I felt. I was on cloud nine all the next day, longing to see you to get everything sorted out, but instead I got home to find James Morgan waiting for me.'

He swore softly as he saw the shimmer of tears the memory evoked. 'Don't cry, sweetheart. Please. If I'd had any idea that James was going to do that, I would have stayed that day and explained what had been going on.'

'But why didn't you tell me later? Why did you let me leave believing the worst?'

He ran a hand over his hair, his face set. 'I was afraid, dammit!'

'Afraid? Of what?'

'Of being in love. I'd seen what it could do to my father. He never got over Mother's leaving him until the day he died, and frankly I was terrified to admit that what I felt for you really was that dreaded emotion called love. It's taken a lot of heartache and a whole lot of sleepless nights to make me come to my senses and realise that losing you would be a hell of a lot worse.'

'Oh, Jordan.' Alex laughed softly, loving him even more for the confession. She leaned over and brushed a kiss along his jaw, moving quickly away again when he turned to her with a naked hunger in his eyes. 'No. Not yet. Let's get this mess all cleared up first, then we have all the time in the world left for... that.'

He chuckled when she blushed. 'Is that a promise? It had better be, because I don't think I can wait much longer. Confession might be good for the soul, but it doesn't do a whole lot for the aches in my body!'

Her heart raced at the rough impatience in his voice, which belied the teasing. 'It is. But first you must tell me how you found out that James Morgan was behind all the thefts.'

He sank back in his seat with a sigh. 'Has anyone ever told you that you're a hard woman, Alex? Still, I suppose I should explain. The signs were all there, of course. The trouble was, I was convinced it was you, so I was too blind to see them clearly. It was only after I found you in the office that second time that I started to have doubts, partly because I *wanted* to believe your claims of being innocent by then. I started to keep an eye on James, and slowly things began to add up, so I back-tracked a bit and did some homework that I should have done weeks before. I discovered that the design faults in the prototype, which we'd been having so many problems with, couldn't have been the result of just bad luck. They'd been introduced deliberately by someone who had to know an awful lot about the engine, and that someone could only have been James. Once I realised that, it all fell into place, and I confronted him with what I knew. He admitted everything—selling the information, slowing down the production by introducing the faults...everything!'

'How awful for you after you'd trusted him.'

'I suppose it's the way of the world. He seemed to think he had a grudge against the company and me, so got back at us the one way he knew was bound to hurt most.'

'What's going to happen to him now? Are you prosecuting him?'

Jordan shook his head. 'No. The damage has been done, so it will serve no purpose washing Lang's dirty linen in public. I've given him an ultimatum to leave the country. I imagine that visit to see you was his last attempt to hit back at me.'

'Will the project have to be abandoned now?'

'Thankfully, no. I've been in touch with our competitors, and warned them that I have James's confession on tape and will use it to blacken their name throughout the engineering world if they continue to work on our design.'

'Surely they wouldn't be able to market it if it was registered to your firm?'

'Not in its entirety, but more often than not it's the concept of a new design which is so important. We need to get it into production before any other competitors to gain the lead in the market.'

'So that's it...a nice tidy ending to everything.' She smiled in pleasure, moving towards him, then stopped when he made no attempt to take her into his arms as she'd expected.

'Not quite everything, Alex.'

A shudder ran through her at the solemn note in his voice. With wide eyes she watched as he pulled an envelope out of his pocket and held it out to

her. She clasped her hands together, staring down
at the slim fold of manilla.

'What is it?'

'Open it and see.'

'No! Just tell me what it is, Jordan...please.'

He opened the flap and pulled out a few sheets
of thick paper, switching on the interior light as he
smoothed them out and laid them on the seat between them. 'It's a formal contract, Alex, ar-
ranging for all the money Mother left me to be paid
into a trust fund for any children we might have.'
He looked up at her, his eyes very level, holding
hers so that she couldn't look away.

'One of the reasons why I haven't come to you
sooner is because I've been working day and night
to push through a deal with a large Japanese
company who were willing to invest in Lang's. I'd
turned them down a few months ago, so it took a
bit of time to interest them again, but it was all
signed earlier on today. I shall retain the major
interest in the firm, but the capital they are in-
vesting will give them substantial voting rights. I've
made arrangements to repay the money I received
from the inheritance into the trust fund immediately. I know I used our marriage to get my hands
on it, but maybe this will partly make up for the
fact.

'As to the rest of the will, perhaps I should have
told you all the clauses but, frankly, there was never
any thought in my head about our getting close
enough to have children; so it seemed pointless.'
He grinned wickedly, his eyes teasing. 'However,
the thoughts are starting to form pretty rapidly now!
But if you stay with me, Alex, and we do have a

family at some time in the future, then at least you'll know that it is because of love...not money.'

'But Lang's means so much to you! Are you sure you aren't making a mistake and won't regret it?'

Jordan shook his head, tossing the papers carelessly into the back of the car before reaching for her. 'The only thing I will regret is letting you slip through my fingers a second time. I love you. You are more important to me than anything else on earth.' He lifted her face up so that he could kiss her with a lingering passion which stirred Alex's senses into vibrant life so that she trembled in his arms. He drew back. 'I shall never let you go again if you agree to stay with me, so can you stand the thought of a life sentence?'

'So you still think I'm guilty enough to need sentencing, do you?'

'I hope you are.' He smiled, his eyes tracing over her flushed face with so much love in their depths that she felt her heart shake. 'Guilty of loving me as much as I love you?'

She moved closer to him, her lips brushing against his as she spoke slowly. 'Oh, I am, Jordan. Very, very guilty indeed!'

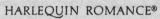